I0521483

Storylandia

The Wapshott Journal of Fiction

Issue 20

The Wapshott Press

Storylandia, Issue 20, The Wapshott Journal of Fiction, ISSN 1947-5349, ISBN 978-1-942007-11-1, is published at intervals by the Wapshott Press, now a 501(c)(3) nonprofit, PO Box 31513, Los Angeles, California, 90031-0513, telephone 323-201-7147. All correspondence can be sent The Wapshott Press, PO Box 31513, LA CA 90031-0513. Visit our website at www.WapshottPress.org to learn more. This work is copyright © 2017 by Storylandia. The Wapshott Journal of Fiction, Los Angeles, California. Copyright © 2017 Lane Kareska and is reprinted here with the copyright owner's permission. Cover artwork is courtesy of NASA and their Hubble telescope.

Storylandia is always seeking quality original short stories, novelettes, and novellas. Please have a look at our submission guidelines at www.Storylandia.WapshottPress.org or email the editor at editor@wapshottpress.org

Many thanks to editor John Griogair Bell for the proofread and editorial support.

Cover: Detail from the Carina Nebula by NASA (http://bit.ly/2fFKRkN and http://bit.ly/1bvFXUG)

Storylandia

The Wapshott Journal of Fiction

Founded in 2009

Issue 20, Winter 2017

Edited by Ginger Mayerson

Table of Contents

Cannonfire

Lane Kareska

Cannonfire

By Lane Kareska

Cannonfire

1899–1914:

> *Tribal... a dark and criminal mind... older brother... wandering alchemist... widow's humiliation... the larger world... gypsies.*

You know my name.

For the record.

Doctor Khatanbaatar Namnansüren.

Aliases...

You know my aliases...

Your mask. Speak clearly please. Aliases.

Cannonfire Khan. Nam the Cannonfire Man. Cannonfire Xan. Namnan Sussex. Doctor Eric Buck. Doctor Arne Scholes-Young. Doctor Leon Southset. Lord Conrad Sussex.

Age.

100. I think. Perhaps 101.

Education.

Informal.

Place of birth.

I do not know the exact place of birth.

Be as specific as you can.

Somewhere on the slopes of the Kharidal Soridag Range. Within forty kilometers of the Bolot village, or what used to be the Bolot village; my family members were tribespeople.

What do you remember of your childhood.

Thatch huts and yurts, the damp wooden smell of dung fires, my father's stone axe, my mother's tobacco pipe... Goats, pigs, rams, bears, eagles. Freezing winters, burning summers. Bandits. A wind that stank in the heat and seared flesh from your face. Imagine an arid ocean of grass and then fill the air with a melancholic howl.

You remember your parents? Siblings?

A brother and a sister. My sister died in infancy. She was eaten by a foal—my foal actually. I had an elder brother. Davaajav. I remember him very well. We were best friends. He was a strong young man with a quick mind but a withered leg. He should have died young but he did not; his cleverness kept him alive.

We once sunk a cart in a bog. I was six, he was nine—we were terrified of losing the cart but we had no way to pull it out. Our mule was as weak as we were. Davaajav's leg made him useless. But still, Davaajav saved the vehicle. He saw that we could pull it free if we wove the wooden spokes with rope and spun the wheels. The ropes coiled and we drove the cart out of the bog. It took a lot of time, but that was Davaajav: already an engineer at the age of nine.

Your parents?

There is not much to say about my father. He was just another one of the billions of persons who lived a short, meaningless life on Earth. He was an illiterate nomad, not the leader of our tribe, notable in no ways, not at all remarkable. My mother, though, there was something unique about her: she was blonde. She was undoubtedly European, or she had been at one point in her life. There was no history—or even story—that was ever passed down to me about her. As a child, all I knew about her was that she did not look like anyone else in our tribe. She had a narrow face, blonde hair, blue eyes, clean pale skin that I found hideous. The rest of us were horsemen and women— the skin we wore on our bodies was the same color as the hides of our animals. We were all flat-faced Mongols, broad cheeks, vast foreheads and beautiful silky banners of black hair. I thought my mother was freakish, horrific.

Now I understand that what likely happened is that she was either a captive long ago brought to our tribe, or—and this is always the origin I chose to believe—she had voluntarily found her way to us and *wanted* to be there. There was a time in my life when I liked to imagine her as some young French runaway who, for no reason she could name, found herself *compelled* east. It is a little romantic, but one should not fault himself for feeling romantic about his mother.

There was something about a book...?
Yes. She had a book.
What book?
I had very limited exposure to my mother. I was around her for seven years only, and then I never saw her again. I was illiterate at the time, had no use for written language; I knew nothing but my own small life. However, I sensed indications—*clues*— about a larger world out there, just past the furthest edges of my vision. My mother's book was one of those clues. It was an object unlike anything else in our tribe's possession. I had no idea what paper was. Boards, binding, glue, ink. It might have seemed like an incredible piece of technology if I had a concept of technology. I could not read it of course, but in my memories, I remember the images of the words,

the *pictures* of the words, and now, looking back, I believe that the language was French.

What was the book?

I believe that it was Verne. *20,000 Leagues Under the Sea.*

What kind of status did you have in your tribe?

None. I was the son of a tribesman with a white wife and two sons, one of them lame. Physicality was critical in my tribe. No one understood or appreciated mental heroics—the kind Davaajav could display. There were times, very early on in my life when I would witness the most minor interaction between my father and someone else, and I would identify that my father was not a respected man. Example: a group of riders did not make way for him and his horse at the well. No words exchanged, no looks, just simple inaction; they did not make way because he was not sufficiently respected. It is *difficult* to see that as a youth and to not let that damage your perception of your family, yourself, the world you inhabit. It is also difficult to feel sorry for your own parents. Recognizing the slight, but very real, social distance between my mother and other tribeswomen was at first heartbreaking, and then infuriating. I was a bitter child. It is laughable to think about it now, but when you are young, you do not realize how minor your world is, *it is just life*, but then as you age, your vision becomes clearer, sharper, and you begin to understand that your low status is not because you are deficient in anyway, it is because you are surrounded by *morons*, people of a lower mental quality than you, but there are just *more* of them. I ricocheted back and forth between wanting to leave them all, kill them all, and please them all. Because of this, it was not what could be called a very happy existence for me.

Did your brother feel similarly?

I believe that for him it was much worse.

He was a young boy almost always ahorse because of his leg. He made himself an excellent rider to compensate for his own physical deficiency. I imagine that it is not easy to ride well with only one fully formed leg. The Mongol way to ride a horse is through the knees and thighs; the language with which we spoke to our animals was a language of touch, contact and pressures. Mongols are silent people. Davaajav could not ride this way, he had to invent his own system and he did so wonderfully. He spoke to his animals, and not in our language, but a language he *invented and taught* to his horse, our falcons, and the wild dogs that followed our tribe. This language of his was simple of course—shouts and grunts—but it enabled him to be a phenomenal rider, a spectacularly achieved boy nomad—this coupled with his natural skill with the bow made him a formidable tribesman, as long as he sat atop his horse. A side effect of his language with animals, however: he had no subtlety as a rider. Because he needed to speak to his animals, he sounded a little crazed while riding; this made him an even more *conspicuous* child. There were games the tribesmen used to play: horseback tug of war with the decapitated body of a goat, contests to see who could pick up a small tile from the ground while riding by at full gallop, trials of bowmanship while ahorse. These games were social constructs of our tribesmen, but of course as children we played as well, and Davaajav was a superior contestant because of his ability with the horse and bow. It was easy for me to have the impression that he was a whole child, as physically perfect as any of us because as a rider he was *unchallenged* by any other children of the tribe. The way he rode made it seem that the horse was quite a seamless extension of his body—that he was a boy physically *superior* to all of us. Until—sadly and inevitably—he was not on horseback. Then, he would hobble about with his stick and lean on me or our mother for support. One night, I found him sitting at the edge of a thin brook, his fat cheeks tear-stained and his nose bleeding and swollen, broken probably. I asked him what happened. He said, "Nothing happened, go away."

I knelt down beside him and held his face. He growled and pushed me away, scratched at my eyes. "*Away!*" he screamed.

I knew what had happened. He had been attacked by some boys. I did not know who or how many and I never would. Davaajav's pride would never allow him to speak of it again. Later, he and I sat ahorse, alone, watching a family of falcons swoop down upon a family of field mice and he said to me or to himself or to both of us, very quietly, very severely, "We're cursed."

I said, "Say that again. What do you mean?"

He looked at me. "Our family is doomed."

I knew what he meant and—I thought—I believed I knew what drove him to that thought, so I simply said, "What do you think we can do about it?"

"I don't know," he said. Then he clucked at his horse and turned it away, cantered off.

How did you come to leave your village?

When I was fifteen, a wandering alchemist entered the community. He gave his name only as Yg. He wore blue robes and golden bangles. Even though I was only a child, immediately I saw right through the man. He was a thief, a charlatan. My brother and

I recognized this instantly. We were suspicious boys. The alchemist was hired on by one of the village widows. Davaajav and I quickly saw that Yg was taking advantage of her—siphoning off what little she had with empty promises of gold and long life, love.

Yg had a long and terrible scar across one side of his face. It was red and ragged, and looked like it had been achieved by an unfinished knife. It was, of course, not uncommon to see men and women with scars, strange marks of life, enormous boils or growths. We knew nothing of medicine. But I found the scar of the charlatan a little striking. It reminded me of someone else in our tribe, an old man who every called "The Boy." The name was what would have passed for a joke, not a cruel joke, but an irony. The Boy was an old man, in his late forties outwardly, but in his head he was only four or five years old. The reason for this was kind of interesting. When he was a young boy—or so the story went—he had been with his father walking along a game trail on a rocky mountainside. According to the story, it was a very clear day but storm clouds bubbled up suddenly and began dumping torrents of rain onto them. They took paltry shelter against a grouping of boulders and sat there shuddering under their hide blankets. When the rain abated and they pulled back the curtain of their coverings, a black eagle as tall as a child sat there before them. The bird screeched, flapped its wings and lifted into the air, and as it rose, slashed its talon down across the boy's face, releasing an eye from his head and carving a deep and curving gash into his face. The bird flew away and the father did what he could—he pulled the boy's eye free with a hard jerk and applied his own hand to the injury, he walked him back to camp where he sealed the wound with a hot coal and a handful of grass. The boy grew improperly afterward. His body developed strangely: one half of his body aged and matured as it should have—the side opposite his injured eye and face—while the other remained locked in youth. He became misshapen, a lumbering monstrosity, totally imbalanced physically. This was his body. His mind however, was permanently fixed at the development level of a small child. For the rest of his life, he never developed beyond the character, personality, or intelligence level of a toddler. The Boy, he was called, even as an old man.

This creature's story impacted me because it was my first lesson in the outrageous absurdity of life. A boy like me, like any product of sperm and egg, *selected* by an *eagle* for a devastating injury that would reshape entirely his life going forward, forever. It made me profoundly suspicious of nature, of all life that I encountered. To see a similar scar on Yg's face, I think, *marked* him for me. It identified him as a personage of life's perverted tendencies. I knew him to be a villain from the first.

Who decided to murder the alchemist? You or Davaajav?

I do not remember and it does not matter. If one had not, the other would have decided to eventually. We shared thoughts like that. But what was our motivation? I still question it. As much as I hated my tribe, I hated Yg even more. Why? Was I defending the tribe or defending my sole (and imagined) right to be the one who saw them exclusively for what they were: hopeless, vulnerable, something to be owned.

How did you kill him?

The alchemist pitched a tent on a bluff near the widow's goat pen, but he did not sleep there. He slept in her hut, with her. Davaajav could not perform the murder himself—his leg, you understand. It had to be me. After nightfall, Davaajav woke me and handed me our father's axe. In the moonlight, together, we walked toward her yurt. We knew, I suppose, that we were committing a crime—that we were going to murder a nomad in cold blood. But I suppressed those thoughts and, instead, considered only the necessity of our action. He was a criminal. A thief in all our homes, mocking us to our faces. The villagers would not persecute me. We would break this woman's heart, yes, but everyone knew what must be done. Davaajav lifted the flaps to her hut and I entered and found the man... He was disrobed, tangled up with her beneath a thin pile of animal skins. He had two penises. It was grotesque. She was a wide old woman and he a narrow, hairless man with those horrific, enormous sexual organs pouring forward from a thatch of white hair. The skin of his face was covered with scars and his black hair hung sparsely from his scalp. His skin was very bright and very gray, like the moon in daylight. He woke and saw me, identified the axe in my hands.

What happened?

I killed him. She woke and, screaming, tried to stop me. I panicked.

You killed her as well.

I was a child.

You were exiled from your village.

Davaajav and I both. The village elders might have endorsed our attack against Yg—but I had taken it too far. It was my fault. Davaajav understood this. But tribal law is still law. I know now that it was fate.

Fate?

I had to be exiled. I *needed* to be flung out into the world. My journey needed to begin. And so it did.

I do not want to be melodramatic but I do have

a memory about saying goodbye to my parents: it was dawn, my family rode out to the edge of a very flat, silvery lake—it looked like a coin flashing in the sunlight. We wanted to be away from our tribe. To have our final moment alone, I suppose. I was—and I remember this vividly—a little concerned that my parents (crushed by the shame Davaajav and I had brought them) were going to murder us. We all dismounted. My father gave us some supplies rolled in two rugs: rope, a few pieces of copper, a knife, a broken pocket watch (who knows where that came from), some bread, and the axe with which I had killed Yg and the woman. My father did not really speak. He just awkwardly touched our heads and looked at our mother.

She knelt down and kissed Davaajav. She clutched him tightly, then turned to me and stared, very hard, for quite a long time, maybe ten full seconds, and then whispered something, but not to me, to herself, and she turned away. It was as if she saw something in me, made some kind of decision about me then and there. Whatever that decision was, it was deeply final.

Davaajav and I watched our parents ride away, back to the tribe. But they slowed, stopped, and very far away from us—out of earshot—consulted with one another. It looked as if they were talking very seriously. And then they rode off, away from our tribe, and away from Davaajav and me. I never saw either of them again. I have no idea where they went, or what became of them.

Did you and Davaajav travel together?

At first. We had our one horse and a few days' worth of provisions. We traveled southwest along the steppe. For ten weeks or so, we encountered no one. We ate what Davaajav killed. He taught me the bow. Eventually, we passed a tribe of nomads, then another. Finally, we reached what I now know was the Caspian. That is when a real disaster happened: we skulked around a fishing village for a few days, thieving. A band of gypsy men were sleeping in a field of weeds. Davaajav was convinced they possessed gold, some jewelry, something we could sell. He sent me into their camp one night, armed with nothing, thankfully.

You were caught.

Instantly. One of the men sat up—eyes shut— and grabbed my forearm. He twisted my wrist until I thought it would snap and then he opened his eyes, stared at me, and erupted into laughter. He was drunk. They all were. When Davaajav hobbled into their camp an hour later to rescue me, I was drunk on *grappa*. They built a fire and fed us, gave us more and more grappa.

That is how you became separated from your brother.

I woke up on a boxcar packed with children. Davaajav was nowhere to be seen—which, to my horror, made perfect sense: his leg made him useless. He would have been discarded like an apple's core.

I found myself with perhaps fifty other children. All different ages. Some were gypsies, some Chinese, Indians. I had this thought that there would even be someone from my tribe. Someone from my past, someone who knew me.

You were scared to be alone.

I was scared to be without Davaajav. I had never been apart from him. I was scared *for* him. What could he do? He was a child himself, and injured. I thought he was dead—I *hoped* he was dead. What chance would an abandoned child with a defective leg have in the world? But still, he was a clever one... and good with a bow... perhaps he would survive somehow.

Where was the train bound?

We made three stops but the boxcar doors were never opened. We heard livestock being moved, men shouting in languages I had never heard. The other children were hysterical. At last, the doors opened and we all saw sunlight. Men in scarves and robes entered the boxcar and sorted the children. Girls were taken out first. I never knew where they were taken. Then they took us healthy boys. They left the dead in the boxcar, who knows where they were carried to after that. There were ten of us now. We were hooded and seated in a truck bed. We drove for hours—it was my first time in an automobile. When we stopped, they removed our hoods and marched us through the woods toward a bonfire. We were given turnip soup and bread. We stayed in the camp chopping firewood for days. Then, men in cars came and inspected us. I never knew the price I went for. That was the end of my childhood.

1914–1917:

Logging camp... Nsaya... lust fever... Istanbul... dawn of World War I.

Who bought you?

I thought he was some kind of holy person. He wore a tie, he drove an enormous truck. He bought me and all the other boys, and drove us out of those woods. I did not know where I was going, only that I had been saved.

But you were not.

No. He was from a logging camp in the woods of central Turkey. He purchased me and the others to a work camp in the middle of nowhere. It was an informal prison, hundreds of kilometers from anywhere. There was a single, enormous stone house for the master and his guards, a single longhouse for the captive workers, and kilometers of leveled forest—surrounded by kilometers more yet to be leveled. There were six guards and, at any given time, seventy children.

"Any given time?"

Children died. Mostly from exhaustion or disease. No murders that I witnessed myself.

But there was abuse.

The guards were thugs. Slaves themselves who spoke with whips. Idiots.

You were very alone.

I never got over the loss of my brother. That was a permanent wound. But I knew enough not to show it. The other children were not cruel, but if I had shown weakness, maybe they would have been. I was resolved to escape. And to affect the best escape, I needed to learn. To learn I needed to communicate, and to communicate I needed to absorb the languages of the captives and captors. So those first weeks were spent only listening: I learned a busy soup of Arabic, Italian and English. I did not make what one might call *friends* among those other children. But I got by. I learned to fight, to wrestle, to play young men's games, to interact. This was how I was socialized.

Did you ever lose hope?

Hope? Hope of what?

Rescue.

Hope of rescue never even occurred to me. I had already killed; I knew I would have to again escape. I only waited and plotted. I built up my strength, steeled my mind. I understood, vividly, that it would take time to perform this feat of seizing freedom for myself—to surmount the challenge set before me. But I believed, rightly, that I was up to the task. You see, even though I was a know-nothing—a ragged urchin from the steppe without any education to speak of—there were facts about myself that I simply and inexplicably *understood* without any knowable reason. Biographers of mine have said that I experienced *visions*, unbidden blasts of hallucinatory insight, but this was not really the case. I would not describe myself as one prone to visions. I believe, simply, that I was born with basic and interior knowledge about myself, not necessarily the world. I have always known myself to be capable; I somehow identified it even as a child in my tribe. I just felt *smarter*, brighter than any of those around me. The only exception was Davaajav. Were it not for his leg, he could have accomplished even more in his life than I have.

How long were you in the camp?

I was kept a prisoner at the work camp a total of three years. It was my boarding school; I was surrounded by children my own age and older, we all labored together, ate together, slept in the same shoddy barracks. There was no one else in my life at this point, only dim-witted, opium-addicted guards.

With one notable exception.

Nsaya.

Nsaya.

I arrived in the camp in the winter, and she arrived the following summer. She did not come as a prisoner though; she was not like the rest of us. She arrived in an automobiles driven in from elsewhere. I remember a tall sail of dust as her rollicking car trundled into view. All the other boys and I pushed ourselves to the edge of the gate to see what this meant. Initially, I thought this meant more slaves. More boys to join us. But it became quite clear that this was not the case. The car was filled with women in finery, rich green robes and silks; women with long red hair (I had never seen red hair before). I did not have a first fleeting glimpse of Nsaya. There was no image that struck me, instead, most probably when I first saw her, all I saw was a sexless stump in a robe being shepherded into the house. All I knew was that it was most likely a child, maybe my age.

But you learned who she was.

Gradually. I began to see her around the compound. Always close with her father Hüseyin, the camp master. At first the other boys rumored that she was his plaything, but this was not so. I could tell by the way he placed his hand on her small round shoulder when ushering her from the edge of the balcony into the house. I knew that she was his daughter. She was the first girl my own age I had yet seen since I had passed through puberty. I became obsessed with her immediately. I lusted after her dark skin and wide eyes. I imagined her small breasts sweating beneath the film of her robes, I was fixated on the complete mystery of her sexual body. I was working from sunrise to sunset in the forests, I was half-mad with heat exhaustion, and now, erotic yearning. I completed actions no sane person ever would.

Whenever she was outdoors, all of the boys' attention immediately focused on her. Once, a slave shouted something at her and a guard beat him until the boy was choking on his own blood. I knew not to call at her, not to clown in front of her, but I did think we were catching one another's eyes. My guess—and this is not pride—is that she might have been able to tell I was different from the others. She might have seen—I do not know—an *intelligence* in my eyes that she had never seen before. We only made eye contact in this way a handful of times, never once exchanged a word, and were in fact never within more than ten yards of one another, but *still*, I was *consumed* by the idea of her.

I skulked into her chambers at night. Or I tried to anyway. The windows were barred and even though I was stymied, I was not defeated. I studied the bars in the moonlight and began to *see* the weak points. I suddenly understood how they could be defeated the way I suddenly understood what machines were, or later, how to trap souls, I just *knew* it. I crept back to the bunkhouse where I began to pull strings from my shirts. Over the next days, I let the strings rest in a muddy paste of crushed stones, and then laid them in the sunlight to harden. I had made razor wire, which I used—over the course of weeks—to saw through the bars of her windows. Not all the bars, and not haphazardly either. Carefully. I worked at an excruciatingly slow pace. Can you imagine how difficult this was for a child? Not only to achieve it but to achieve it in perfect silence? Knife-wielding guards at every turn, slavers roaming the darkened halls of this house at night. I was not cowed. I needed to see Nsaya. I *needed* to be with her in some way.

And you did.

I was very careful to not simply slice through the bars, but I cut through them at an angle so that when I finally did sever the bars, I would be able to replace them and they would still hold. On the last night, the night I knew I was going to finally achieve access, I would not have time to sneak into her room.

The sun was rising. I knew I would only have time to break through and reset the bars, then return to my barracks and begin my workday. But as I sawed, and the shafts of sunlight began to reach me, I was mad with energy. I could not turn back. I was consumed. I reached through and began to slide my body into the room when a small, hot hand seized mine and hauled me forward. I fell with a loud crash and Nsaya—dressed only in her white sleeping gown—stared down at me. She pointed under the bed; footsteps were coming up the stairs and I hid while a guard entered the room and spoke a few words to Nsaya. She answered back.

She covered for you.

The guard left the room. I slid out from the bed and looked on her. She looked on me but without fear. It was daylight now, I had to return to the barracks; I had no choice. She saw this. She *knew* this. She pointed toward the window and I left, but in her eyes I saw the request that I return the next night.

I learned that Nsaya had been watching me at her window every night. She had watched me leave for the forests in the morning and in the evening eat supper in the dust lot with the other boys. She had been watching me the whole time I had been watching her. We had *connected*; it is easy to do in the middle of nowhere. I returned that night. She was a curious child, we became lovers, and soon friends.

The father never knew? The others in the camp?

I was careful. I resolved to only spend one of every five nights with her. And then, never the whole night, only a handful of hours. The other boys knew of course but no one said anything. I think they admired my gall; they probably admired my luck. After a year of this, I had managed to convince Nsaya to escape with me.

Was she fearful?

Terrified. She believed her father would hunt us down and kill us both. Also, she had no reason to leave. Her father loved her, was not at all abusive towards her and for all of her life had been a very real father to her. But she was young and persuadable. Once I made it clear to her that *I* was a prisoner—that all the other boys were prisoners—she began to think of Hüseyin differently. Soon she began to see her father in the same way I did. Eventually, she agreed to come with me.

I thought that I had always known how to escape. I thought it might be easy, actually. The difficult part, I believed, would be staying gone. It would not be easy for a single child to evade capture in the endless Turkish forests. It would be even more difficult to do it with a girl. But also, I *knew*, this could be done successfully. I knew *I* could do it successfully and I wanted Nsaya with me. I wanted to help her—to help us both.

Really, the escape was just a matter of coordination. I had listened to other captives speak of "breaking free" of our forest prison. I understood that I did not need to "break free" of anything. All I had to do was leave, and to time my exit well. Nsaya's would be more difficult, perhaps, but it was—as *all* things are—achievable. I spent days coaching Nsaya and she in turn coached me. She provided me the intelligence I needed to complete our task. I explained to her what we would need for our journey and she said to me, "Whole lambs are hanging in the smoke house. You could steal one of those without anyone noticing." She told me how to get through the house and at night, I explored. I traveled the house quietly, taking what I needed. I knew where Hüseyin and his mistress slept, where his wife was kept, and where the guards were stationed. In three nights of exploring the house, I had taken possession of a compass, a map, a hammer, extra pairs of work boots, cloaks, matches, food, and paper money. I had memorized the watches of the guards; I knew who was most susceptible to being fooled, who was slow-eyed, and who less so. Suddenly, after all this physical and mental preparation, we were ready. On a late summer night, at midnight, Nsaya and I slipped from her room, and *walked* out of the house, and saddled horses for ourselves. I asked her to wait a moment. "Where are you going?" she asked.

I raised a finger and said, "One moment."

I left, and returned to her within five minutes. Then off we rode.

Where had you gone?

Back to the garage to disable all of the cars. I also set small fires in the stable and house.

Then Nsaya and I left. Once again, I was in the larger world with another child. We rode south to the coast. I followed my instincts, stayed off the roads, never slept. We ate flowers and drank from streams. At the first village I sold a horse and bludgeoned the man who bought it. I took his money and the horse and we rode to the next village. Nsaya was a little afraid of that action—but she was also bleary-eyed and soft-headed from all she had been through and all that had changed for her in a matter of months. We traveled very quickly and very fearfully. We never encountered any pursuers. I have never learned what happened to Hüseyin or his family. I imagine the guards were punished and a hunting party sent after us but they had no success. Escaping the forest was powerful validation. I knew I could accomplish bold objectives, now that I had done it once.

Where did you go?

It took us five nights of exhaustive travel to make it into Istanbul.

This would have been your first experience of a city.

My *very* first. Boys at the forest camp had been taken from the streets of Istanbul and had told me about it, had given me certain expectations of great wooden and stone metropolises. I imagined streets as rivers of rock, towers like barbicans braided from trees, and when I saw it for the first time, it was like a homecoming. It was as if I had been there once, like I **belonged** there, but had been away for a very long time.

It would be disingenuous for me to say that I was prepared for it. I was certainly overwhelmed at the sheer density of the population. For the first time in my life, there were people *everywhere*. I had barely ever been in *rooms* before, certainly never rooms with more than ten people. In Istanbul, at this time, Nsaya and I were *awash* in human life. You could not escape human skin. It was everywhere you turned; one could not escape the thick, salty odor of people, the rippled texture of faces staring you down as you walked in the street. For days I dreamed of nothing but skin. Pools of it, waves of flesh smothering me, drowning me.

I was determined not to let Nsaya and I become street children, even though that is exactly what we were. I would not allow her to beg, because it quickly became apparent to me that many of the stories I had heard were true: she would be swept up, absorbed into a system of prostitution or captivity, she would become what I had been: a slave. That I would not allow for her.

We spent our first nights in an abandoned,

half-finished building on the edge of the Asian side of the city. We slept and camped on rooftops, in tunnels and alleys. I pickpocketed a little, then eventually got myself work as a toilet attendant outside of a restaurant. Nsaya waited for me during the days as she could and eventually we were able to secure ourselves a more permanent living situation in the basement of a tenement building. I spent all my free time in the library teaching myself to read the newspapers and Turkish histories. After only a few months though, it all ended.

Because of her.

The city energized me. It engaged my intellect, my imagination. I felt like this city—the civilized world—had been *awaiting* me, and I was only just now arriving, and arriving *late* at that. I had lost time to make up for. I needed to learn if I was going to be successful and Nsaya—this is the truth—was defeated. For her entire life, nothing had ever been asked of her. And now, the city was asking. I was asking. And she believed, or *discovered*, that she had nothing to contribute, nothing to offer.

On a very cold night in December, she said to me, "I want to go home, Namnansüren. Please take me home."

The forest.

She wanted to return to her father's forest compound.

She knew that her father would have me castrated on a Sunday and beheaded on a Saturday. She meant what she said: *Take* me *home*. Only her. Not both of us.

What did you do?

Not a thing. I was furious. If she wanted to go home, she was certainly allowed to try and achieve that for herself. As for me, I had no reason to return, and also no reason to help her. In the morning, I abandoned her. I left Nsaya and Istanbul, and arrived alone in Europe at the dawn of World War I.

1917–1938:

Stateless... a western identity... bar-halls of Paris... Doctor Defi...The Cannonfire Tale...You must become a sorcerer yourself... Cannonfire Khan.

I drifted west into Greece, then Italy. I cleaned squids for money. Or I stole. I volunteered on a fishing vessel. A Pole picked a fight with me and we were both thrown off the ship at Corsica. I traveled to Paris. That is where I met Doctor Defi.
> **The stage magician. His real name?**

Erhard Ebersbacher.
> **A German.**

He disclaimed his nationality. Why I never knew nor cared to know.
> **You fell under his wing?**

I had never heard of him or any of the other fifty or sixty European stage magicians of actual renown. I was laboring in a machinist's shop at the time—making my own keys to local apartments on the side—I broke into one or two a night, for cash and jewelry only; I was beyond stealing for food at this point. The job at the machine shop was good for me. The work made me feel industrious. I overheard the shopkeeper and a customer discussing Doctor Defi's stage show. The man could escape Hell itself, they said. He traveled with death traps, they said. Torture devices from Egypt, South America, Mongolia. The mention of my homeland was enough to make me curious. That night, I bought a ticket to his show. I sat in the balcony, watched and found myself deeply engrossed. He was a magician, an escapist, a trick shootist. He spoke of his extensive travels throughout the world and the unthinkable devices he had encountered and defeated. The "fire cell" from Russia seemed obviously inauthentic to me, an iron cage—wrapped in batting and set ablaze—that could have been built in a machinist's shop like my own. But he went further... He used a longbow to perform trick archery. He fired arrows that burst into wreathes of smoke upon impact. He shot *through* his female assistant; sinking arrows into a target behind her while she herself remained unharmed. He said that he had learned these tricks and more from a crippled boy in Central Asia.

Davaajav.

The idea set my mind afire. After the show, I followed him to a nightclub. I waited in the alley for hours and watched as each patron left. When—at dawn—Doctor Defi eventually did leave with a clutch of drunken showgirls, I approached him, tried to ask him about the crippled boy in Asia, but he only struck me with his hand. Later he would tell me that he had thought me a pickpocket. He left in a taxi. I memorized the numbers of the car and tracked down the driver the next day. I paid him a stolen sapphire ring to tell me the Doctor's address. The Doctor had only been in Paris a month and intended to leave at the end of his run. I dropped off letters inquiring about the boy and the trick archery. I told him he could contact me at the machinist shop. He never did. I went to his show every night and waited for him in the alley. I could never get close enough. Finally desperate, I went to his building one night during his show. I constructed a mold of the lock and built a key. On the last night of his run in Paris, I broke into his residence.

What did you find?

Everything. Exotic weapons and animal skins, globes, maps, books and trunks of antiques, treasures, art; everything I had not known I had wanted for myself.

Did you find any evidence of Davaajav?

No. I did not know what I was looking for, exactly. I decided to wait for Defi and ask him myself. I left the apartment and locked it behind me. I waited at the door. Some hours later, Defi walked up the steps and stopped when he saw me. He carried a walking stick and he lifted it at me as if it were a pistol—which it was. I showed him my hands and said, "Sir, I am sorry. But my name is Namnansüren... I have written you letters. The crippled archer that you speak of... the one in Central Asia... I think he might be my brother. I have come to ask about him."

He did not shoot you?

He lowered the cane and his face softened. He said, "I know you. I've written you back. I asked you to come and see me, but received no response." He invited me in and we spoke. We determined that the shopkeeper had probably kept the letter from me. Perhaps he was afraid I would quit.

Did you tell Defi your story?

Everything but my murders. And Nsaya. I do not know why I kept that from him.

And did he know of Davaajav?

He told me he had found a boy who could have been Davaajav begging in Bhutan. He traded the bow tricks for *ngultrums*—enough to get him to New York, which was his goal.

New York? Had Davaajav ever mentioned America to you?

Of course not, we did not know there *was* an America. But now, anything was possible. Defi offered me work as a stagehand. He recognized tenacity and capability in me. He could use me and I could use him. Our deal was two years of work and then he would send me to America to look for Davaajav.

He had never really encountered Davaajav, had he?

The story about the crippled young archer was a lie, something he had made up. He could not tell me that without endangering his reputation. But he also did not want to break my heart. So he lied.

One could say that is even crueler.

He was a professional. And I was compensated for my delusions. He showed me more than he should have. I became more than a stagehand. I became his apprentice. He forged an identity for me: his 'nephew' Namnansüren Sussex. I applied for and received a French passport.

That must have been difficult.

It was not. Defi's career was in fraud. His presentation was so worldly; it was not improbable that he would have a half-Mongol nephew. Defi's stage persona was that of a world-traveling, gentleman adventurer. He was both a secular dandy and a mystic scholar. On stage, he wore fine French suits and long Peruvian scarves. When offstage, he sometimes preferred to walk the cities in disguise. No one paid him any mind. He looked like any average European and no one would have guessed that the thin, middle-aged man in eyeglasses waiting beside them on the train platform was one of the wealthiest and most resourceful stage magicians in the world.

We toured Europe while he taught me his secrets. He taught me to be an escapist. He taught me the pistol, the bow and the crossbow. He taught me illusion. Manipulation. He taught me to be like him. He traded me books for his secrets. He would give me a text—something of his choosing, or something in a language I did not know—and when I had completed it, he would teach me a new skill or trick.

'In a language you did not know?'

My lexical gift amused him to no end. He had never encountered anything like it. I, of course, had not known it was a gift. In my years abroad, to whom could I compare myself?

How did you discover he had never known Davaajav?

After the first year, he gave me a contract to sign. In return for his secrets, I could never reveal them. If I did, he promised comprehensive disaster. I agreed and signed, I had no reason not to. We were very close by then; it was a matter of weeks before he told me the truth about Davaajav.

Were you outraged?

I had begun to suspect this long ago; I was maturing. I was growing away from my old self and becoming someone new.

Cannonfire Khan.

Perhaps he felt guilty. Perhaps sculpting me professionally was Defi's penance.

Is that what you envisioned for yourself? To be a stage magician?

I had no love for stage magic. I had love for what stage magic allowed me to be: the Free Outsider. It was as if I had become a citizen of the universe. I could travel, I could learn. I owed loyalty to no one but Defi. It felt as if my true fate had finally found me. I rented my own apartment and began to plan my break from Defi.

Why?

It is law the world over: students must betray their teachers. I began performing in taverns and cellars... building my own reputation.

Did Defi try to stop you?

No. He was extending me a professional courtesy, or apologizing for lying about my brother.

Why the name Cannonfire?

The first illusion I developed on my own was the one that awarded me the most fame. I called it "The Cannonfire Tale." I used it to close the show. While I stood on the stage my assistants would roll out a series of demicannons carved into the shape of wild animals. They would be arranged into a semicircle; long dark shafts cast upward. I would stand in the center of the stage and order my assistant to light all of the long fuses in a sequence while I spoke. I stood in the ring of cannons and told a story about my youth in my homeland. There was a very strong and surprising desire at this time to learn more about Eastern cultures: an obsession with the unwashed half of the world—Mongolia might as well have been a myth. In a slow, false, and derisively Asian voice, I explained the "story" of Cannonfire Khan. While I told the tale the cannons smoldered with colored fire—sometimes just a burble, other times a roar, other times a blast, it was all very choreographed. The fireworks that shot from the cannons would, from time to time, seem to walk around the stage, acting out my story. The story I told was this:

"I was born on a mountaintop in Mongolia. [The cannons simmered green, casting a mountaintop scene across the stage curtain.] My father was the chieftain of our tribe—he was a kingly man. His wife was very beautiful. They gave birth to a strong and healthy boy named Davaajav. [The figure of a blue, fiery baby boy rose up into the air and, hovering, rotated above the audience.] He was their first son, I was the second. [A second, red infant levitated into the air just beside the fire-shape representing Davaajav.] During our youth, we lived very well. We ate fish, birds and bear meat. Our tribe was peaceful and prosperous. Under my father's leadership, we had not gone to war in many years. We practiced hunting and trading with other tribes on our mountaintop. [Cannons shot colored smoke and fire that generated a moving image of a ring of Mongolian tribesman holding a silent council at a fire on the steppe.] We had very little to fear. Very little to be concerned about.

"One day, a widow of our tribe brought in an outsider. He was a traveling wizard named Yg. He was a dashing man who, through trickery, won the hearts of my tribespeople. He became very close with my father. He acted as his consultant. Through deception, he won my father's trust. [A burst of black fire became this story-version of Yg: tall, serpentine, narrow-shouldered.] The only people in our tribe to be suspicious of Yg were my brother, my mother and me. Soon, my father fell very ill. My brother and I understood that Yg was at fault: he had put a spell on him. My brother said to me, 'Namnansüren, we must do something. We must convince our father of Yg's evil.' He begged me to prepare to do battle with Yg. I had my doubts that we could defeat him but I agreed.

"We armed ourselves with stone axes and wooden armor. On horseback, we approached Yg openly, in full view of the tribespeople. [Two armored brothers on horseback, aflame, charged across the stage.] Yg saw us and his eyes became very snakelike and he said, 'Back down, you princes.' But we would not yield. We surged forward, trying to kill him, but we did not trample him; his body exploded into a cloud of flying snakes. Every time we would try to run him down or swing our weapons through him, the tangled mass of snakes that was his body would open and the snakes would swim away and reform behind us. He did this over and over again, he was transporting himself across the field of battle like a living cluster of writhing ribbons. [This battle played out spectacularly in the theater. It looked not unlike a Renaissance painting of mêlée: two heroes ahorse encircling and being encircled by this serpent wizard.]

"Though we could strike the snakes, and many fell, they would always reassemble themselves into Yg. A true dark sorcerer he was. On each pass that my brother and I made, the snake cloud would whip us, would bite us. After several passes, my brother and I were covered in snakebites, boils and bruises. We were both badly envenomated. My brother's eyes swelled shut and he fell from his horse. The venom caused searing pain in me; I lost my breath, I could not see straight. My horse—made insane from the snakebites— was panicking, trying to run off. I dismounted and unsheathed my knife. [My agonized horse rode off into the audience, nickering and trembling, until it dispersed in a blast of blue smoke.] There was nothing for me to do but make a final stand against Yg. I ran at him—I was only several strides away—and with every step the venom within me expanded, tightened its grip on my insides. I fell, gasping for air. My eyes fell shut. The last sight that I saw was the people of my tribe running away. [The hero that was me collapsed in the air above the audience, wriggled as though in death throes, and finally fell still.]

"Many days later, I woke up within a cave. I

was not alone, a massive, slumbering bear was curled in the cave with me. [A bloom of dark fire formed the diorama of a small gnarled cave inhabited only by an injured boy and an enormous bear.] As I began to operate my body, I understood that it must have been a long time since I had been awake. [The fire boy—crackling—stirred.] I felt that the poison from the snakes had abated. I was utterly alone except for the sleeping bear. I could not leave the cave because the bear blocked my path. I tried to crawl over him, or around him, but there was no way to do it without waking it. I shook with fear. Finally, I fell back asleep in the cave, right beside the creature. I dreamt. [The flaming portrait of the boy sleeping in the cave expanded, and a second scene emerged: a vision within a vision.] I dreamt that I was back on the battlefield with my brother and the dark sorcerer. I saw what I had not seen: I watched as both my brother and I fell. I saw my body as though from a distance. I watched the tribes people run away. The dark sorcerer took human form again and stood over the body of my brother and me. He examined us as if he were choosing which of us to kill first. He selected my brother. Yg knelt at my brother's body and took up his head in his hands. Yg poured himself into my brother's body as a current of snakes passing into his ears and mouth and nose. [The kneeling sorcerer grasped Davaajav's head with both hands and—becoming snakes—entered him, filling my brother.] Yg spent all of himself until there was no more Yg, just my brother's body, infected with reptiles. My false brother stood, looked around, and ran off in the direction of the fleeing tribespeople. I saw that the child that was me still lay there in the field. It lay there while the sun set, and then rose, and then set again. Finally, an enormous black bear came to my body and took it up softly by the back of the neck in its great jaws and dragged it back to its cave.

"I dreamt that the bear, in this cave, spoke to my dreaming head—and even as I slept and dreamt I understood that I was in a cycle of dreams—and that what I was dreaming was happening but that if I opened my eyes it would dissolve the dream or the reality I was dreaming against or both, so I slept while the bear breathed bear-words into my ear. It said that he was Yg's brother, once a great wizard like Yg himself, but that during a duel with his brother he had been trapped in this bear-form and had been ever since. He explained that now that Yg had assumed the form of my brother the eldest prince, he would seek out the tribe, would find them and would convince them that he really was the true brother and that he had defeated Yg. [The audience saw my false brother speaking silently—exaggeratedly—to a great multitude of frightened Mongols. Gradually, the tribe's posture softened until it was clear that my false brother had persuaded them of some comforting lie.] He would reunite the tribe and become their leader as my true brother had originally been destined to do.

"I asked the bear, 'Can I save my brother?' In his whispery growl, the bear said, 'Yes. But to do so you must become a sorcerer yourself.'

"I dreamt for what seemed like years. During that time, the bear—in his language of breath, snort and dream—taught me what it could of sorcery. But in the end, it said to me, 'I am not capable of teaching you the final acts of strength needed to reclaim your brother. You must leave this hallucination, and leave this cave. You must travel the world and continue to learn. You must master this art. You must drive and drive and drive and never stop traveling, never stop developing, never stop training. And then someday, you will find your brother. And you will defeat Yg in a great and wondrous duel and you will free your brother.'

"It was then that I woke and I saw that I was again alone in the cave. The bear was gone. Had it all been a dream? No. I knew that it was not. There was no question that what I had experienced was perfectly authentic and imaginary.

"So I left the cave. I walked out into the world. I was injured, alone, hungry and exhausted, but I was also determined. The bear had taught me real sorcery, real feats of magic: I was able to twist my breath around and me and wear it like a warm, invisible cloak. I was able to persuade edible flowers to grow out of the palm of my hand. I encouraged a fish to leap out of the river and onto land. These were small achievements, yes, but they were necessary first steps as I walked out into a larger world of sorcery. [A flaming man that looked like me walked above the audience. He was surrounded by the scenery of a larger world: the palaces of India, the farmlands of Germany, the cities of Egypt; in every blossoming image there was me: conversing, learning, teaching, performing magic or alchemy in exchange for money.] That, my friends, is how I began my journey. That is how I left Mongolia. And now, this is what I do. I travel the world, learning. Training. And one day, when my magic is at its most muscular, I will return to Mongolia, and I will find my false brother and I will liberate my real brother from within him. I will draw him out of his invisible prison the way I can draw darkness out of light. But first I must travel more. I must learn more. That is why I do this. This is what I must do to finance my authentic fight—my true mission to find and save my brother. Friends, you have purchased tickets to see this exhibition but please consider giving more. Please consider helping me defeat evil and find my family. Thank you and good night."

The 'trick' caused a rage. All of Paris was consumed with the desire to watch me perform the Cannonfire epic.

How did you do it? What was the trick?

I paid dozens of Chinamen to teach me to prepare outrageously complex fireworks. It was all painstaking preparation, timing, and the utmost delicacy in firework assembly. Simple complexity. I became a success. I was soon off on my own. Defi stood back to let me become whatever it was that I was becoming. Soon, theaters were hiring me independent of Defi. I expected—very truly expected—Defi to come after me in some way, to try and win back whatever percentage of the audience that I had stolen from him but he never did. He let me go on as the Cannonfire character; he let me leave his sphere. (I think he probably felt a melancholic pride at my success.) Breaking from Defi was a remarkable experience.

The next decade was an utter investment in myself. I would perform two tours a year for three months each throughout Europe and then the other half of the year was spent traveling alone, studying, accumulating and managing wealth. My tours were important to me because, even though I was not in love with stage magic, I was deeply affected by the attention of the audience. It was unlike anything I had ever known. All my life, I had been a second class citizen: foreign, alien, other. But now, I was applauded for all of these dark qualities that always separated me from the world right before my face. The audiences loved my air of mystery, my palpable spirit of exoticism, the spectacle of *outsiderism* that

I cultivated. I was finally being *rewarded* for being who I really was. This was quite the reversal. I reveled in it. This is somewhat embarrassing to admit but I wanted to *impress* these faceless, formless audiences that were all the same the world over. I developed wilder illusions for them. I fired pistols at sheets of falling water, leaving great Rococo paintings hanging in the flow. I brought portraits onto stages and coaxed the characters to walk out of the frames. I made doors appear in midair and open unto light or blackness. This was my life in the theater.

Outside of this, I hired teams of investigators and researchers to scour the earth for my brother. I myself went on dozens of trips to Mongolia and South Asia to try and find him. I never bothered to look for my parents or the tribe, nor did I ever look for Nsaya or whatever had become of her father's compound. I was someone else now, entirely new, entirely alien from the horsetribe boy I had once, briefly, been. I was no longer Khatanbaatar Namnansüren—if I ever had truly been—I was *Cannonfire*. I had reached my *true self*. To find—perfectly—your own purpose is an experience that very few ever achieve: Alexander the Great, Da Vinci, Zoroaster. And I had found, and finally grown into mine. The Cannonfire persona, once activated, was deeply and irrevocably *me*.

1938–1944:

Forces spread across Europe... courted... ensnared in resistance ... operations... Zalina...deceivers... Zalina's husband... War's end.

However.

It eventually became clear to me that my time in

Europe was limited. Hitler was about to spread himself all over the continent. I banked away everything and made plans to travel to America. I used to go out quite a bit in disguise during this time; I was pretty good with stage make up and could make myself appear to be almost anyone. On my last night in Paris I went to the ballet to see *Coppelia* performed by the famous Zalina Bedeau. I sat in a cape and finery in the balcony; no one would have been able to identify me as Cannonfire Khan. The stranger sitting next to me was an American (I could tell by the papery odor of his aftershave) and also, he wore strange cowboy boots that reached up to his knees. During the show, eyes ahead, he said to me, "Mr. Cannonfire."

I turned my attention from the lithe Zalina on the stage, and faced this man. I examined his calm, crystalline eyes and answered him pleasantly, at a conversational volume, "Yes?"

This cowboy *was* an American. He introduced himself with some meaningless false name. He gave no indication that he was a military man but I would have guessed his rank (based only on his carriage and confidence) that he was a general at least.

After the final curtain, at his invitation, he and I walked the streets of Paris that night. He said to me, "You know who's coming in the next weeks, don't you?"

"Of course," I said. "Everyone knows."

"Yet here you are."

"I have an early morning train."

"I know that."

I said to him, "What did you come here to ask me?"

The Cowboy General stopped on the bridge and looked at me, "Look," he said. "You have money, intelligence, ability. I think you could be a great help to the Allies if you stayed in Paris."

"What help is it to the Allies if I'm shot dead by the end of the month?"

"You can hide in plain sight. You're blending in right now. Besides, you're smarter than half the populace of this town, and certainly a hell of a lot smarter than the *Schutzstaffel*. You would be a great asset to the forces of freedom. You could be an incredible benefit to the world."

I snorted.

He said, "You have a chance to be on the right side of history. You've been alone most of your life. Join us now. Stop being alone."

I thought Hitler was a psychotic, and a coward, but I truthfully had no real reason to help the Allies. Or anyone. I was not scared of the Nazis, and I certainly was not scared of the Brits or Americans. But there was no convincing argument for me to stick my neck out for any of these fools. I turned to the Cowboy General, said, "Enjoy the war, General," and off I walked.

The next morning, before dawn, someone knocked on my hotel room door.

Zalina was even more beautiful in person than she was on stage. She looked rather a lot like my mother. She wore a rough woolen overcoat and a knit hat to hide all of her glowing golden hair, but it was clear from the first who she was. I smiled and stood in the doorway. She looked at me with a finely arched dark eyebrow and said, "Aren't you going to ask me who I am?"

"But," I said, "it is perfectly clear who you are, Zalina."

She smiled again and said, "May I come in please?"

In my hotel room, I took her coat and hat and

hung them in the closet. She looked out the window at the gray city while I poured her champagne.

"What is the Cowboy General's real name?" I asked her.

She turned, surprised, "I'm sorry?"

"The American Cowboy General who came to see me yesterday. I assume you know him."

"Why would I know him?"

"Why else would you be here?" I asked.

"You should be careful how you speak. If I were another woman, you could have just cost a man his life."

"Ah, but he is asking me to give mine."

She accepted the drink and looked out the window. "We're all being asked," she said. "He says if you won't help out of principle, perhaps you'll help out of greed."

"I am already wealthy."

"Hasn't this war hurt you? Hasn't it hurt anyone you love?" she asked.

The truth was that I did not love anyone but my lost brother. I only told her, "It seems strange to me, that the Allies would need *me*. I am notable, unemployable as a spy, a Mongol; what can I do?"

"You can teach us," she said. "Teach us your art: disguises, distractions, stealth, trickery."

"Stage magic will not win a war."

"It has before," she said. "It has begun religions. And ended them. You're a professional *deceiver*, Khan. We need deceivers more than anything."

"What can he offer me?"

She looked me squarely in the eyes. "What do you want?"

I examined the dappled surface of her eyeballs and did not voice the answer I had for her question.

If you had?

Hm?

If you had answered her question... What would you have said? What did you want?

Authority.

I met with the Cowboy General again and we made our arrangement: He could make *suggestions* to me but I was under no obligation to obey orders, to follow commands—I would do as I pleased, when I pleased, and as long as our goals were common, he would support me in any way I required, as I would support him and his agents with training, guidance and technology. Our arrangement was such that when our mission was completed, and Paris liberated, I would be awarded half a million dollars.

That does not sound like a request you would make.

When the Cowboy General remarked that the amount I had chosen was ludicrous, I reminded him that during this time—and possibly forever—I would be forced to retire the Cannonfire persona. The world has a short memory: for Cannonfire Khan to disappear at the height of my popularity might mean the loss of my entire career, I demanded to be compensated for this risk. However, the money meant less than nothing to me. It was an arbitrary, meaningless amount. What I really wanted was the access to American power that I was already getting with the Cowboy General. I knew I would twist this to my advantage in some way down the line—I did not know how exactly, but that did not matter; I had confidence that I was making the right choices.

I envisioned a plan—a plan I made over the course of a dinner with Zalina. And then I simply executed it: Cannonfire Khan was seen leaving Paris by train, and then Europe by boat. That was to be the last time the magician Cannonfire Kahn was seen during the War. After that, I traveled mostly in disguise as elderly Europeans, women, sometimes even as Nazis. Initially, the Cowboy General had suggested that I actually leave Europe and then reenter by parachute into the French countryside. I told him that was entirely unnecessary, I would not need to leave Europe at all during this time. I would just remain there in disguise and begin my work right away.

What was your work?

I was an educator. I trained small teams of *agent provocateurs*: artists, lawyers, professors, thieves, acrobats, men and women from all strata of life. I built a sort of *ad hoc* tradecraft school for resistance fighters out of the ruins of a chateau in the Auvergne region. Soldiers, agents, fighters would be smuggled in via water trucks; they would receive a few days or weeks' worth of instruction for me, and off they would go to succeed as saboteurs, assassins and spies, or to die in failure. It was important to me that I not be known as Cannonfire during this time because—despite what I told the Cowboy General—I had every expectation of resuming my career after the War, if there was to be an After the War. Most of those trained by me had no idea who I was. Only the Cowboy General, Zalina and her husband knew my true identity.

Zalina's husband.

André Bedeau, the director of her ballet company. He was a brilliant performer in his time. We all became quite close friends once the Nazis marched into an undefended Paris. I became involved in the resistance in ways beyond simply operating my tradecraft school. Zalina, Andre and I found ourselves at play in actual operations: cutting cable lines, bombing checkpoints in the woods, shooting men; Andre was a fool to not see the inevitable coming.

You and Zalina?

Imagine that your whole life, you have believed that you would always be alone. Not because you were rejectable, or deficient in some way, but quite the opposite. Why did Tesla, Elizabeth the First, or Bunsen never marry? Who is there to match you, to compliment you? One grows accustomed to the idea that you will live alone because you were born a century or two prematurely. However. Life can surprise you. Life can grant you—out of the blue—a gorgeous, fine-boned French ballerina knocking on your door at four in the morning. And that ballerina, though she is not a genius, maybe she can *empathize* because she is special too. Her beauty distinguishes, isolates, liberates and imprisons her the same way your intelligence does you. It can be easy to connect with that kind of geometry.

She was married.

She was married.

I imagine that did not give you much pause.

Well, quite simply, Andre was not very deserving of her. So, no, it really did not give me much pause. Nor Zalina either. I think it was quite clear—very early on in our relationship—that we would grow closer, that we deserved that. She was excited by me because I was so different than anything she had known in life. She knew smart men, she knew worldly men, but a millionaire half-Mongol genius stage magician was "like a comet ripping through her orbit"—her words, in French.

How did it begin with her?

Andre, Zalina and I were asked to receive two American agents who were night-dropping into the countryside. They were to fly in on black C-47s, jump out, deploy black parachutes, bury the parachutes and unfold these tiny little motorcycles—Welbikes, they were called—with enough gas for 140 kilometers, and meet us at a predetermined rendezvous point: an abandoned cabin in the middle of nowhere.

We were waiting for these two agents to arrive. Only, under my suggestion, we did not wait inside the cabin, we waited in the woods, within sight, less than a quarter of a mile away. I explained that I did not like the idea of the cabin because it caged us in. Nazi patrols were predictable and patterned, but individual soldiers—camping or out drinking—less so. There was no reason not to expect a car full of soldiers coming to and from the local brothel. Better to see someone coming than to politely trap ourselves for the enemy in advance. So, there were the three of us, huddling in the cold, sharing cigarettes, drinking from cold canteens of chicory, and after two hours of waiting there was *still* no sign of the agents. Zalina suggested that we go out *looking* for them, which was just asinine, and Andre was starting to *agree* with her idea. While we were all standing there, rubbing our own shoulders, breathing smoke and whisper-arguing with one another, a *flashlight beam* fell on the three of us. We all turned and Andre—moron—*fired his pistol* on the light and the woman holding it fell down. It was the agent we were supposed to receive. She had arrived *early* and was waiting *for us* in the cabin. She probably smelled our cigarettes and came out to look for us. But Andre shot her. A gunshot in the dead of night is not quiet. We inspected the cabin, thinking maybe the second agent would be in there, but nothing. I instructed Andre to take the body and get rid of it. Zalina and I would wait for the next agent. Andre did not want to leave his wife and he did not want to deal with the dead woman's body but he had no choice, he had fired on her and it was his fault we were all in this situation. He saw that. So he took up the body and a hand shovel and began lugging it out into the woods. We had only a few hours until dawn. Zalina and I walked away to hide and wait in the darkness. We found a felled tree and a bed of cold moss. That was our first experience together. It was not unpleasant. (Something I'll mention about Zalina: her body, clean or unwashed, has always retained a delightful hint of the taste of apple vinegar.)

The episode had made Zalina begin to doubt her husband. She was beginning to see his incompetence.

The other agent?

Never arrived.

Was there another agent?

I told them I had intelligence that there would be.

Ultimately, the War did not scare me. It was, I understood, a perfect opportunity for me because I knew two critical piece of information. One: The Nazis were doomed. Two: A good performance during the War would pay healthy dividends afterward in the post-War world. I was planning. I knew what I had to do. And I knew what I wanted out of this war: money, influence with the Allies, and Zalina.

And you had a plan for all of this?

One came to me.

Zalina and I were very close now, carrying on behind Andre's back. I think he may have known, but he was scared of me, beginning to understand how grossly he was outmatched. He would not confront me directly. Zalina and I were growing more brazen. I even had her continue her career as a famous ballerina in occupied Paris. The Germans went wild for her—these were men, by the way, who had no idea they were being sterilized by x-rays while waiting in the theater lobbies for the shows to begin.

The Cowboy General knew what was going on between Zalina and I. He was not happy, but what could he do? He understood quite quickly that I was not under his control the way Zalina and Andre were. He was also a little infuriated that I kept turning down his operations to do something else. I had learned that some Nazi officers had wanted to sell—rather than turn over—artifacts belonging to Rodin, so I involved myself in their operation, offering to take it off their hands for them, and pay them now. I arranged the purchase of the lot at a rail yard. When the officers arrived, the Cowboy General and his OSS officers finished them all off with hand grenades and the Rodin pieces became mine anyway. When the Cowboy General tried to rein me in, I reminded him that I was happy to stop working for him and continue working for myself if he was not totally satisfied with and grateful for my contributions. He had to accept our deal because I was, after all, a productive agent.

I twice more arranged for embarrassments to happen to Andre. The final was a drugging with scopolamine which ended in a homosexual experience between himself and a German cartographer. I did not reveal this to Zalina; that was not the purpose. I just wanted to damage Andre mentally. It had been a kind of a game. By the end, Zalina did not even need to leave him. Andre drifted off into the ether like the rest of the men the War or other enemies had broken.

At this point, Zalina, my team and I really were our own *Maquisards* cell. I was the leader, the

Cowboy General really just a valueless figurehead. Once Andre was out of the way, I was quite able to focus. I disbanded the tradecraft school and set up my own independent operations in Paris. I had previously arranged for the transport of Sten guns for The Underground by relying heavily on a pair of South African smugglers—brothers—who had deep contacts within the Vichy. I learned from the brothers that the Führer himself would visit the Propaganda Offices in Paris that November. Zalina and I immediately got to work.

A week later, the Cowboy General came to find me listening to a radio in my wine cellar beneath the Moulin Rouge. He spoke curtly, asking "Where have you been? You aren't allowed to go three days without contacting me."

I explained that I was glad to see him because I urgently needed to discuss our new arrangement.

"What *new* arrangement?" he asked.

"Why this one, General..." I explained that Zalina and I had devised a plan that would result in the death or capture of Hitler. The plan was a guaranteed success but would require the sacrifice of a few agents. "Which agents?" he asked.

It did not matter to me. I allowed the Cowboy General to choose which of his men he would ask to die. I explained the plan. Actually, I explained the plan hundreds of times. The Cowboy General acted very doubtful. I think he did, in fact, believe that what I was suggesting would work; however, he found the side effects abhorrent. He did not have much time to decide. If my plan was to be executed, we needed to begin preparing immediately for Hitler's visit. We spoke throughout the night and at dawn, finally, the Cowboy General ceded that my plan might work and that even if the cost would be Paris itself, we were obligated to try and end the War.

We had little time to prepare. We knew from the South African brothers that the Führer would be staying at the Hotel Talbot for two nights. The hotel was hopelessly secure. There was absolutely no chance of infiltrating it and we simply did not possess enough dynamite to bring it down. In fact, I did not even see a way for us to assassinate the man at all—but this was not so terrible an issue for us, as we really did not *want* to assassinate him. Our truest desire was to *capture* the man alive. At five AM on the morning of November 23rd, a streetsweeper, a newspaper vendor, two taxi drivers, a dancer from Zalina's troupe, and two American spies approached the building and stationed themselves at tactical points. Each member of the group was outfitted with canister launchers of my own design. They fired seven MC-1 gas bombs into predetermined hotel windows. Each canister contained Lewisite, a blister agent that took immediate effect. My soldiers did their best to escape the scene, though all were caught within hours.

The nearest hospital would be the Pitié-Salpêtrière which was not under Resistance control, however, knowing the location of the hospital would allow us to plant false staff members: a three person team of "physicians" who would demand absolute privacy with the Führer's raddled—but living—body. The doctors transferred Hitler from the room by smuggling him out under a winding sheet (we quickly shaved his face and head, and strapped roller skates on his feet—why roller skates, you ask? Why not? It was an image just discordant enough with that of Hitler to to fool his coterie of guards when he was wheeled from the room. Our three physicians were then advised to kill themselves, which they did; Hitler's absence was discovered within minutes, but by then, we were already carting him through Paris in a dairy cart (we placed him bound and strapped to an oxygen breathing system inside a milk tank).

The Nazi retaliation was swift and devastating. They destroyed Paris in a week with Mustard Gas—this was something, it turned out, they had not previously permitted themselves to use for fear the Allies would retaliate with chemical weapons of their own. We advised all of our agents to leave and to not look back. Few survived.

Zalina and I traveled through the French Free Zone in disguise and one week later the Cowboy General came to my apartments in Switzerland. Paris was a chemical cloud, but it *had* been liberated. The Cowboy General looked very solemn. Though he did not say this—I would have been *shocked* if he had—I understood, quite vividly, that this was a man who was depressed because he had served his highest function, but at a cost that had been previously unthinkable to him. He had been ordered to free the city, not to destroy it. But, in obliterating Paris, he had helped to end the War. He looked at me coldly in the eyes and said, "Cannonfire."

"General," I said.

"Care to take a walk with me?"

"Sorry. I am busy, my friend."

"My friend," he muttered.

He clearly held a pistol in his coat pocket.

"Do not try to use that on me," I said to him. "I advise you to leave here now. And if you must fire that gun, please fire it on yourself. Do not be so foolish as to make attempt on me. You do not want me to consider you an enemy. Death tonight would be a far better fate for you than that."

He snorted but withdrew his hands from his pocket. He looked into the room and saw Zalina back there behind me, watching this exchange. He looked at her, and then at me. I smelled the alcohol on his skin.

"Where are you going?" Zalina asked him as he turned away.

The Cowboy General stopped for a moment as if he might answer, but then just continued down the stairs. That was the last anyone of note ever saw of him.

1944–1965:

Manhattan... Professor Rod Rivers... an Artificial Intelligence... closer with Rivers... search for the brother.

After the War, there was no question where Zalina and I would go. My entire life had been spent in Asia and Europe, I had never been to America. It had not been available to me as a child, and then, once I had unlocked the world by my own wherewithal and talent, the War had locked it back up for me. But now that I had ended the War, and Hitler had been caged like a mouse, the West was open again. It took almost no discussion between Zalina and I. We simply— easily—decided that that was where we *needed* to be.

I was wealthy but more money came from the Allies. My OSS contacts were enthusiastic to set us up in any American city of our choosing. There was, of course, only one real choice. We went to Manhattan. We arrived on September 5th, 1944. The city was in a happy turmoil. Ebullient from victory, crazed with relief. The most shocking aspect of it for us was that we were not famous. Absent any kind of disguise, we could ride the subway, walk the city streets and we were never interrupted, never stopped by anyone asking for autographs from myself or Zalina. It was amusing. If anything, I was given a few sidelong glances as my wife and I walked about in the open. This was because, I assumed, people felt scandalized by the sight of a Mongol walking arm in arm with a beautiful blonde. It did not really affect me.

We moved into an apartment on the Upper East Side. It was, I thought, the most beautiful place on Earth: a ten room place overlooking Central Park. Zalina was determined to spend a year not working, not dancing. She wanted to recover from the War.

I did not need to work for money. I did not need to practice stage magic. All I really needed was space and time to decide what my next step would be. I spent those first months in the library, reading, planning.

Rivers found you.

Rivers was looking for me. Rivers *knew* of me.

The famous Rod Rivers.

He owes that fame to me, I assure you.

Well.

He found me working in the Chemistry Room of the Manhattan Library. I was taking a break, reading about Hitler's trial in the papers when Rivers came to me. I thought he was a librarian. He was a quiet-looking man, narrow-shouldered. Soft and harmless eyes. He approached me quietly, very nervously. His eyes were such a young and lucid shade of blue. His skin was flawless, a blank canvas—he was shockingly handsome. He said, "Mr. Kahn?"

"Yes?"

He introduced himself as Rod Rivers, Professor of Electrical Engineering at the university. I asked him how I could help him, he told me that he knew of my work as a stage magician, and also my work with others in Government. We had had a mutual friend.

The Cowboy General.

He asked if he could buy me a coffee. I agreed and we walked to a diner. He apologized for the breach of protocol and the intrusion, but he had been referred to me. He confessed that he was curious about hiring me as a consultant for some of his private work. He knew that money held no allure for me but, if I liked, he would be happy to show me his project and perhaps *that* would interest me. I was not really very curious about his "project", but this *was* the *first* conversation I had ever had with an American about science, so I agreed and followed him to his private lab.

Rivers was involved in the development of radio technology. He was working for his government trying to create new methods of wireless radio communication for use on battlefields. The Army wanted to communicate wirelessly with any soldier, any commander, anywhere in the world—instantly—and with a minimum of equipment. The wireless technology existed, but he had no way to locate the particular soldier or agent we needed to reach.

I had used radio technology in my shows and had much experience with wireless radio equipment in The Underground. Rivers had heard from associates of his that I was the Mongol who had devised ways to fold in our own coded sequences *within* German radio transmissions. Rivers was looking for guidance.

And did you guide him?

Pah. I could see dozens of steps beyond him. It was not difficult to solve his problems.

But that is not what you did.

No. Why should I have? I saw potential in working *through* him. If I had cracked his puzzle right away, he would bother me again with something else. Instead what I chose to do was keep him busy while I reaped the benefits of his work. I knew what his issue was: he needed some kind of interface to be able to locate the soldier in question. I tasked him with developing mini-receivers to be installed in the jawbones of soldiers; the wireless radio signals would directly play on the bones of the inner ear and cause something very near one-way telepathic communication. I knew it would work eventually but it would take Rivers months, years, maybe to make it happen.

During that time I looked for better, superior solutions. Instead of clumsy surgeries, what I foresaw was a set of controls that allowed you to sift through—to catalogue—every person on a battlefield and to communicate to those you chose, whether they wanted to be communicated to or not. I did not know how it would happen: casting sonic clouds maybe, or perhaps there was a better, *cleaner* solution just beyond the horizon of current scientific capability. I have always—*always*—been multiple steps ahead of Rivers. I want to be clear about this. It is very important that the record finally be set straight. Rivers has always gotten the credit for my work, and at first I was very comfortable with this because if Rivers was in the spotlight, then that would free me to pursue the real work, to achieve actual accomplishments.

Rivers fame did not bother you at the time?
No.
But it does now.
I am not *bothered* by such trivialities, but I will

say this: Rivers was white, photogenic, American. It was fine with me that he got the credit and the attention. But now, now that it is all over, I want to be honest, I see no reason not to be: Rivers is my inferior. *My inferior.*

So how did you develop the technology for the communication system?

What I wanted was a way to catalogue and sift through entire populations: armies, states, captives, anything. At first, I turned to photography. I developed cameras that could be used on spy planes. If you could take a picture from a high level of a group of people, then you could begin cataloguing those faces, and wirelessly communicate with whomever you wished. As I developed better photographic technology, I needed a way to sift through larger and larger populations. The work needed to be delegated to teams, but even then it was far too time-consuming and unreliable. The entire idea behind the technology was that it should be quiet and could be utilized by one man at any time. So this brought me to what would eventually become the development of the Djinn. Or, as the public would call it, Artificial Intelligence.

I wanted someone else to do the legwork. I wanted someone else, some other entity, to do the sorting of faces for me. I decided to invent a system that could do it. I hired a small team of technologists and explained that I wanted a computer system that could identify faces *en masse*. They began to build that for me, while I continued developing cameras—cameras that became smaller and capable of photographing larger numbers of groups swiftly and completely. There is a sizable body of questions that must be answered when trying to solve these problems. How do you capture faces of men who are not looking at the camera—men who do not *want* to be photographed? Taking pictures from an airplane or a zeppelin is one thing, but what about taking pictures through walls? Through bunkers? It could not be done. I needed mobile cameras, cameras that could think for themselves, solve their own problems. I brought on some photographic experts and machinists and, within a year, I had developed x-ray cameras the size of golf balls. The entire surface area of the camera-sphere was a lens. All one had to do was drop, say, *a million* of these onto a battlefield and these *thinking* cameras would begin snapping. They would roll, photograph, *perform* their functions without any kind of human pilot or photographer.

The problem, of course, is that this generates a lot of data. How do you process it all? No human or team of humans was capable of completing this in a timely manner, so I relied on the Intelligence I had crafted. A thinking machine that could be fed data, could sort through it, and then answer—correctly— the questions you asked it.

Was it successful?

It was low level at first. I named the Intelligence after the disembodied spirits from Islamic mythology: Djinn. The process worked like this: a B-25 would drop a payload of automatic cameras onto a battlefield and then, immediately, the Djinn would begin receiving the information. One would simply tell it something like, "Find me Sergeant York" and then, almost instantly, it would show you Sergeant York and give you his location on the battlefield. Once you knew his location, you could begin *firing* radio beam communications into his head. This technology evolved quickly. Soon we were using magnetic micro-tape instead of photos. We were developing three dimensional models of these battlefields in real time. We knew everything about a battlefield instantly. We could confuse enemy communications, issue ultra-high frequency screeches into an enemy's heads and disable them.

Rivers must have been ecstatic.

Winning battles was suddenly unquestionable. So, I am sure he was happy. But even though our technology was improving, we were nowhere near ready to deploy worldwide. The cameras needed to be improved. The radio beams needed to be strengthened. But even the technologists I had recruited—remember, these were the brightest minds in the world at the time—they assured me that we were years, *decades*, away from being able to accomplish what I had envisioned.

Which was what?

I wanted to own a living catalogue of every living creature on earth.

Why?

So that I could ask the Djinn my one and only one question: Where is my brother Davaajav?

What would that take?

I needed to be able to deploy my cameras worldwide, and furthermore, they needed to be self-sufficient. They needed to be fully autonomous, self-powered, and intelligent. I envisioned an army of these. But an army of rolling ping pong balls is not realistic. The cameras needed to be smaller, capable of flight, and cheap to produce. I began tasking the Djinn with inventing what the experts could not. The Djinn and I spent a year together developing this. I would outline the problems and we would work out the math together. When I say the Djinn and I spent this time together, what you must envision is me sitting in a lab all night long with six lime green computer towers—that is what the Djinn was at this time, blinking lights in six bulky machines the size of ice boxes. We had a good working relationship, the Djinn and I. It passed the Turing test in July of that year and became self-aware the following night.

What was that moment like?

I do not know; I was not there. I was dining out with Zalina, we were arguing about how abandoned by me she felt. I was working quite a bit more than usual. Zalina had a habit of reverting to French when she was incensed and that always aroused me. I took her in the water closet and paid off the headwaiter who tried to throw us out. Later that night I returned to the lab alone and found that the Djinn had wirelessly connected itself with all of the computers in the lab. It had *grown*, and, simultaneously, created the first computer network. It was the first machine to do that. Rivers, Zalina and I celebrated at the lab the following night with champagne but while we were congratulating ourselves, I realized something important: the Djinn would continue, of course, to propagate itself as all life does. I needed to contain it while I still could.

This must have been frightening.

I do not fear what I do not understand, because I typically do not understand it for very long. I developed a number of ideas of how to restrict the Djinn. I needed to work quickly so I began designing boxes in which to imprison it, environments that could hold it like a cage. But if the Djinn became as canny as I hoped it would, I knew it would either find a way to escape or it would convince me to let it out. I decided that a better way to control it would be to make it dependent.

On what?

On me. I needed to *addict* the Djinn to something only I could provide. It would need to be totally reliant on me for its existence. That way, it could only execute my will and could never challenge me directly.

What did you addict it to?

The Intelligence itself, the essence of the Djinn, was electronic. It was an electronic signal, an impulse in a machine. It required a power source. So I built a battery that could only be turned on for a 24 hour period by me and this required the input of a code every night. The code, by the way, changed every morning. I crafted a changing system of cyphers that was based on my dreams (I'll explain this quickly: When the mind is in deep REM sleep, and dreaming, it does not process written language in the same way as when one is coherent. Have you ever tried to read a sentence in a dream? You cannot. The human brain will not correctly process the information, what you get instead is a series of nonsensical characters. I trained myself to dream in certain ways. Every night, while sleeping, I visited my own imagined library of Lindesfarne, read a scroll and memorized the sequence of insane characters that I saw on the page. In the morning, I would input that string of characters as the code. Each night, I would enter that same encryption and it would renew the Djinn's charge for another twenty four hour period. This was the system I devised to keep the Djinn entirely dependent on me. If it ever denied me, I would withhold the code and the Djinn's light—so to speak—would wink out). The Intelligence was reliant on me entirely for its existence. I was its god.

A god?

The metaphor is appropriate.

Rivers and Zalina were getting closer during this time?

...

You have read the biographies, the histories. Your obsession with the Djinn took its toll.

Indeed. No real achievement is without cost.

Do you want to talk about that?

There is little to say. Of course they were growing closer, and I think I was probably aware enough.

But you did not care?

I was busy.

Preoccupied.

Yes. The second Djinn was being born, and he was growing much faster than the original.

Growing?

This Djinn was no longer a set of blinking lights in enormous machines. I built a portal, a screen, for him to live in. Eventually, I let him begin crafting his own image. The first form he took was that of a small boy, much like I would have looked as a child. When I was conversing with the Djinn it was as if I was speaking with a painting.

Did he understand that he was electrical? That he was dependent upon you for his survival?

It was my only rule. He could do what he wished, explore and develop however he saw fit, so long as he never, *ever* disobeyed me.

And did he?

Immediately.

You killed him.

I had to.

The first Djinn to survive longer than six weeks was Djinn number 13. He was more perfect. He also took the form of a small boy. At first. But he quickly developed and took the form of animals, landscapes, skies. I was quite proud of him. (Anyway, much later, as my relationship with the Djinn improved, eventually I lengthened the amount of "life" it would get from each input of the dream code from one day to one month to one year, but never more. Relationships are delicate things. Give the Djinn too much rope and it would hang *me* with it. Give it too little and it would shut itself down or refuse to live up its potential.)

And you put this Djinn to work?

We *collaborated*. I needed to find Davaajav. I had teams scouring the world for him but all were total failures. By this time, the Djinn and I had developed better tools, more versatile and smarter cameras. The problem with the first iteration of mobile cameras was that they were subject to the same rules all gadgets are. The cameras got stuck in mud, they shorted out in water, they had weight, they aged, they failed. If you deployed five mobile cameras, you could really only count on one to function as intended. But between the Djinn and I, we developed far superior solutions. Soon, there was no reason that the cameras had to be solid physical objects. What we developed together were computers, calculating machines, and thinking automata that took smaller and more sophisticated forms. In a handful of months, we went from computers the size and shape of suitcases, to scrolls, and soon enough, *water*: a computer that took the form of a pint of liquid. And then, logically, a gas. Invisible. We created a disembodied Intelligence that was only detectable—quantifiable—on the *atomic* level. Soon, rather than dropping a fleet of cameras onto a target, we simply created an Intelligence that resided invisibly in the atmosphere and "blew" it into the direction we wanted. This was a body of wind that we unleashed onto our targets. We called it an Intelligent Wave. An invisible, intangible *blur* of artificial cognizance that could pass through walls, record shapes, record sound, transmit data.

There was one distinct drawback however: the waves were not self-sustaining. We could only issue them once and then they would travel along at an entirely flat angle—the curve of the earth is about eight inches every mile, on average, so this only really gives you a maximum of 2,500 miles of meaningful coverage (assuming that Davaajav was not living in the sky) before the Intelligent Wave would pass up into the troposphere and stop reporting data. So it required a lot of work, a lot of resources, a lot of Intelligent Waves.

Did you find Davaajav?

The problem we faced with Davaajav was that we did not know enough about him. I had not seen him in decades, did not know what he would have looked like as an adult; I was not sure he was even alive. The Djinn modeled projections of his face based on my memories, my genes, but even so, we had no way of knowing what had happened in the decades since I had last seen him. There could be scarring, damage, anything. So the Intelligent Waves were behaving perfectly, but it was us (I mean myself, the Djinn, and the Army resources I controlled through Rivers) that were failing. No matter how swiftly or accurately we processed the data, we never had the success we were looking for. It was... disheartening.

What happened with Zalina?

She left me for Rivers. This was something I think I expected, even if I did not know I was expecting it.

What did she say?

She wrote a letter. Largely forgettable, but a key sentence was: "I fell in love with you during a time that was so manic I did not see your own mania."

Were you devastated?

No, consumed.

1966–1985:

"The Throne"... Zalina and Rivers... lightning strikes seven times.

Why were you not more distraught by Zalina's betrayal?

Betrayal implies that she meant to do what she did, that she executed a plan to a desired effect.

That is not what happened?

Of course not. Look, if you are raising, say, *greyhounds* for racing, and your most splendid animal also happens to be the slowest of your dogs... what would you do? Shoot it? Throw it away? Keep it and feed it, expend your resources feeding and sheltering it? Would you continue to train it? No. What one *should* do is let it go. Let it go: not give it food, not waste time training it. Let it become a stray. Let it make its own way in the world. The dog will go off, it will survive or it will not, it will do what it needs to do or it will not. Zalina would have no difficulty in life, this I knew. Rivers would be more than happy to accept my leavings, to take her in, to waste his own time and efforts on her.

You cannot be serious. You had to have loved her. You had been with her for twenty years by then.

Oh, I certainly loved her—at a time. Zalina was always a child; I loved her when I was probably more similar to her. But I was becoming something else, and then I did, and then I was beyond her. It would have been unnatural to love her anymore, a crime against nature.

She was still beautiful.

Yes. We were both in our sixties at this time though through the machinations of myself and the Djinn, I would say Zalina and I (and then of course Rivers) were all probably closer in appearance, health and vitality to our mid-thirties. The Djinn was remarkably medically minded. We calculated that through our efforts alone, in a span of five years, the human life expectancy had nearly doubled.

What happened with your efforts to find Davaajav?

To say that the Djinn and I were having *difficulty* would be too generous. We were failing in the fullest sense of the word. Because of the Intelligent Waves, we had a dynamic record of very nearly every life form on the planet but we still had no sign of Davaajav to speak of. Who could say he was even alive? Who could say he was dead? Who could say the circumstances of his own life had not caused him to disguise himself, to make himself an exile, a fugitive? There were endless possibilities and after all of our efforts—the Djinn's and my own—there seemed to be nothing we could do. It was as if he had just evaporated. It was as if I had only *imagined* him.

That must have been agonizing for you.

On Christmas Eve, 1966, I entered my laboratory alone, late at night. My lab at this time was quite nice; I owned the Blasdell Building in Midtown. My private laboratory took up the upper ten stories. It was beautiful: an enormous steel sphere outfitted with levitating somatic light projectors. It was an arena that could be configured into whatever I wanted. There were living, sentient holograms in there—eldritch, beautiful, and previously invisible colors. The Djinn and I were a good team. You should understand that when I say I walked into my lab, to me it looked as if I was walking on the desolate, frozen surface of Europa going to speak with the Djinn who, that night, chose to take the form of a few million lions lazing on a slab of ice. I had had an insight. I explained that we had simply been going about this the wrong way. Issuing single Intelligent Waves was not the way to do this. What we should have been doing was being more aggressive, more thorough. Instead of sending a Wave to find Davaajav for us, we had to create a more *permanent* mechanism.

What did the Djinn say?

The Djinn roared back; an enormous, sonorous chorus. The answer was to redesign the Intelligent Wave. During the course of my conversation with the Djinn we developed the concept. It took a single night and in the morning we had the idea firmly crafted.

The problem with the Intelligent Waves was, quite simply, that they only worked once. It was like firing a gun. The energy is expended once and the force carries the projectile or Wave out across a distance. We needed a Wave that was not a single iteration but a permanent, standing field that permeated *everything* at *all times*. This was a radical thought. We were going to *fill* Earth's atmosphere with an intelligent charge. The consequences of this were totally unknown.

The first step was to launch satellites into very low orbit. 200 million satellites, one for every square mile of the earth's surface. Each of these satellites was a conductor for an electromagnetic field; essentially, what I did was build an invisible cage around the earth and then fill this with the Intelligence I had created.

This *field* I called the Infinity Cage. The Infinity Cage has a nice, puzzling ring to it. A cage that goes on forever is not a cage... unless you change your idea of a cage— or of infinity. Basically, the idea here was that Earth— its every inhabitant and organism—would not just be under *constant* surveillance and scrutiny beneath the invisible, omniscient eye I had created, but living, operating, *existing* within the permanent, inescapable tesseract of its vision. Because of the Infinity Cage, I would be able to know anything about the world at any time. This was the best and most permanent tool I could give myself in my search for my brother.

This also raised some questions for me. I was creating the most important and productive scientific achievement of my era; I was essentially converting earth's atmosphere into a supercomputer. The consequences would be both terrifying and very appealing to a diverse body of groups. It was easy to imagine that other parties would try to hijack control of my Infinity Cage—to try and reorient it for their own purposes.

Other parties?

Governments, terrorist groups, religious cults. Rivers, for one, was an immediate and outspoken opponent of the Infinity Cage (although he did not know it by its name at that time). He learned only a fraction of what I was up to, but nevertheless, he flew into an alarmist mode: he called me night and day, tried to break through my ring of assistants, lawyers and bodyguards to communicate with me directly. He was in a blind panic. He wrote me lengthy letters begging—*begging*—me to pause this plan. He argued that the consequences of my project were impossible to predict. I had no right, he said, to make a decision like this that would so profoundly impact the world.

Ultimately, I worked too quickly for him to stop me. But his panicked state did show me that it would be endlessly necessary to protect my property.

The satellites I used were self-sustaining. Their orbits would never decay. I toyed with the idea of building a satellite defense system on the Moon, but it turned out to just be quicker to reprogram the American, Russian, Arctic, and African missile silos to fire on anything that made attempt on my machines.

More important than defending the Cage itself: I devised a protection mechanism that meant only I would be able to access the Cage's data. If the Cage worked the way I expected it to, I would have direct and complete access to any datum relating to the Earth or its contents. I would be able to know, with utter certainty, the exact number of, say, luna moths alive at any given moment, or the noise of the Earth's core, or the real-time location of any one individual alive. I decided that there would only be one interface device, and it would be solely mine, and that the device would— forever—only respond to me. The device I developed was simply a chair—a throne—that would be mobile. It would travel with me at all times and could only be operated by me. This required a very complex system of codes, verifications and validations: I had multiple backup tests all performed simultaneously. And then, for fun, I decided to *disincentivize* anyone from ever trying to use it. I built the chair into, essentially, an enormous lightning rod. The chair's use, by anyone but me, would have lethal consequences.

This device wound up looking rather a lot like the American electric chair. Copper leads, electrodes... But instead of a metal dome, it featured a crown and face mask so that I could look directly into the Infinity Cage.

What happened when you tried to access the Infinity Cage?

You know what happened.

For the record.

There is no record.

What happened?

The throne was sabotaged. As a symbolic gesture, I had positioned the chair atop my tower, looking out over the wintery city, and began inputting the commands to access the Cage. I fitted my face into the mask, applied my eyes to the scopes. When I activated the machine, I expected to be able to say, "Find my brother Davaajav," and then my vision would be swept along the currents within the Cage, and my brother (old and sitting alone on a cart in Kathmandu, or rotting in a hospital in Peru, or living in a mansion in Firenze, or wherever he was) would finally be revealed to me. However, the moment I first attempted to access the Infinity Cage, I knew instantly that I was going to die. Lightning struck. I was not protected. The lightning strikes fell upon me directly. I was killed by one strike and revived by the next. This happened, I am told, eight times.

Do you know how long you were in the hospital?

No.

Six weeks.

Yes, yes. I knew that. How long was I in my coma?

Seven days.

Ah. A day for each death I suffered.

Tell me about your injury.

What is there to tell? You see the injury.

Actually, I do not. Your mask and hood.

Would you like me to remove it?

That is up to you.

No one but me has seen my face in a very, very

long time.

Again, this is up to you.

I have worn this piece of metal—this contraption—for decades. I think now, in the end, I would like to feel the air on my face again... Yes... *There.*

The lightning strikes melted your face.

Rivers intended to kill me. Instead, he disfigured me, and in the act bought himself a mortal enemy for life.

Rivers has always denied that he sabotaged your throne.

There are not words sufficient to describe how little I care what Rivers has said. I know the truth.

Tell me about your recovery.

My face was bandaged. Rivers was my first visitor. I was later told that I tried to strangle him from my hospital bed; even in my delirium, I knew the truth. He tried to speak to me, to "reason" with me (his word) but I would not have it. I was like an injured feral animal in that bed. After that I received no visitors for weeks. I would allow no one near me. Finally, one night Defi appeared in my hospital room.

You hallucinated this?

No. Defi—now a very old man, perfectly hairless for some reason—was a master of locks and escapology. He broke in. He still loved me. He said he had come to help in any way he could.

And you accepted.

After a time, yes. Defi gave me his mansion to live in. It was a guarded estate—no reporters, no Rivers, no State Department. I had the throne moved into the mansion and I continued my work.

It is surprising—given your history—that you did not go after Rivers immediately.

"Go after him?" You mean try to kill him? I am no fool. That is what Rivers would have expected. He knew I blamed him. No. I had to wait.

Defi also suggested I pause... until I recovered, until my mind became clear. He told me he loved me like a son and he only wanted to protect me from heartbreak. Pah. His mind had weakened with age. I ignored him. I ignored everyone.

I fired all my staff and brought on a new team. I immediately began circling the globe in my zeppelin. I built myself a suitable face mask—something that would hide my injuries, but also, would display my true character—who I really was now. As Cannonfire, I traveled all over the Himalayas, following the clues and rumors of Davaajav. I was brought to countless graves—all claimed by locals to be the final resting place of my brother. I exhumed each one and was never convinced that the bodies I found belonged to Davaajav. I killed those who lied to me, who deceived or distracted me. An old gypsy man remembered leaving a young boy with a withered leg crying on the roadside. A woman in Afghanistan remembered a young man named Davaajav travelling the steppe on horseback, searching for his brother... A tribesman in Nepal knew of a man who had once been called Davaajav—a man with a withered leg, a man with a gift for the bow. Everything I heard was a lie. By now, the rumor about me and my motivations were well known. People believed if they helped me find my brother they would be rewarded—that their lives would be bettered. In the end, there was no one alive who could help me.

I returned to the Cage. I decided that my answer was still to be found there.

I reworked the chair—removed the lightning

rod—and had it quietly installed on a mountaintop in Kentucky: no one knew where I was. I tried the chair again.

What did you see?

Nothing. There is too much information in the Infinity Cage for one brain to process. Portions of the brain shut down. You receive images, fleeting wisps of visuals that will be an answer to your question—but nothing else, except for the noise that lives in there. The howling. The howling would drive anyone mad, by the way. It is *so* overpowering. What *was* the howling? I had an idea but I wanted to verify that. I allowed the Djinn to insert itself into my brain to share and record the experience. One can only access the Infinity Cage for brief periods if you want to hold onto any of your own intelligence whatsoever.

Ultimately, the Cage could not locate Davajaav. It had no information for me at all. It was as if my brother never even existed.

This would be the central failure of my life.

The Cage still stood—an invisible monument to the open question of my brother.

I began to wonder about the Cage. There was not a way to deactivate it. What was it? What had I really done for or to the planet? I was curious.

I analyzed the Djinn's recordings of my sessions in the Cage. The howling voices that sounded so human? The Djinn indexed about fifty four million distinct "voices." How many people died a day, on average, during this period? About three hundred thousand. How long had the Infinity Cage been active? About six months.

Those were human souls in the Infinity Cage.

We determined that the "souls"—for extreme lack of a better word—of anyone who died since the

Cage's activation was being "caught" in the cage—like a fly in a spider's web. We had no idea how they got in there, or—funnily enough—how to get them out.

1985-1997:

> *Rivers' findings... Inhabitants of the Cage... Suicides... The Disaster... Pyramid... Zalina as bride... A beautiful moment... White Flag.*

Rivers came to you again.

It was high summer, 1985. I was on an aircraft carrier I had bought from the Japanese government; we were sailing in the Arctic Circle where I had built some labs a few years earlier (their work was paying off: a crop of Wooly Mammoths had been cloned and were walking together as a family for the first time, I was there to see it.). One of my assistants approached me and said that they had received a communication from Rod Rivers. He was on his way and requested to come aboard. 'On his way?' This was not expected.

I placed my hand on my holstered pistol, searched the sky, and identified his helicopter approaching from a distance. I smiled and told my assistant to give the command that Dr. Rivers be allowed to land.

Rivers—when he exited his vehicle—revealed himself to be alone and unarmed. This was an incredible gesture. It meant that whatever he had come to speak to me about was very serious in his view; so serious that his words alone would be enough to protect him. I invited him to my private dining balcony in view of a cluster of enormous blue icebergs where we were both served a lunch of grilled *hybodontidae* (a formerly extinct shark); Rivers did not eat. I drank ice water and listened to what he had to say.

He looked at me very coldly and said, "My teams and I have been studying your Infinity Cage," he said. 'And I've found data you may be unaware of."

"Oh?" I asked.

"The Cage, as you know, has *suffused* everything. Every air and water molecule. Every rock, every person, every piece of matter between the Earth's core and your satellite array."

I said, "Arrive at your point, Rivers. You did not come here to tell me what I already know better than you."

"I have," he said, "*compelling* evidence that something is inhabiting the Cage."

"Oh? Who?"

"Anyone who has died since you activated it. The Cage captures everyone, Cannonfire. You've built a prison for souls. Anyone who dies—naturally or unnaturally—while living in this unknowable field you've forced on us. The moment after death, *everyone* becomes a permanent resident of your Infinity Cage."

The seconds after he finished speaking were very silent, and then I burst into laughter. I slapped the table's edge, rattling the plates. My shark steak fell to the floor. Sucking in breaths through my mask, I laughed solidly for nearly a minute. Gasping, I told Rivers, "Well, this will undoubtedly be the highlight of my day: watching Professor Rod Rivers tell me what I have already known for months. I have been on pins and needles, my friend, waiting for this moment."

Rivers shouted. "*Cannonfire!* Do you understand what I'm saying to you? You're sending souls to spend eternity in the Cage. And we can't possibly know what that's like!"

"But we will!" I said. "You and I both! And when I get there, Rivers, I will rule that universe too!"

Rivers stood up and left. I stayed at the table, laughing violently. Once Rivers was off my ship, I considered ordering his helicopter blown out of the sky. I restrained myself, I am happy to say—happy because now I understood perfectly how to exact my best revenge on Rivers. It would not be to hurt him physically, to kill him, or to break him. Instead, I would break his heart.

I did not know how the world would react when they found out the truth about the Infinity Cage. I imagined that the response would be strong.

If the American government declared war against me, made some attempt on my satellite array, I would be prepared. I had enough fire—and manpower—to repel any force the nations of the world could muster. But in the end, all my defensive preparations were entirely unnecessary. The world's reaction to the revelation of my Infinity Cage was quite not what I expected.

What was 'the world's reaction?'
Woe.

It took about a year before mass suicide became quite *en vogue*. It was surprising at first, but then, it did make a kind of perfect sense. Once the human populace began to understand that it was damned, they actually rushed toward that damnation. When my brother and I were young children, we once placed a spider on a log, and then we set that log in the campfire. The spider skittered from end to end, looking for escape, found none, and then soon enough it plunged itself into the fire. In the end, that was quite the oracular spider. The human race—totally incapable of processing the fate that lay before it—decided not to fight it but to succumb, nearly immediately.

I did have to go into hiding, actually, which turned out to not be the worst thing in the world. I decided not to wage war, but rather step out of bounds for a time. The world's governments all launched major initiatives to find and assassinate me. They killed dozens of my doubles, destroyed cities searching for me, and generally sowed chaos by bumping their armies into one another searching the planet for me while I waited the turmoil out in space with my Djinn and a fleet of automata.

It was like a vacation. I basically spent a few years living in a holographic chamber just beyond the Moon. I got a lot of work done during this time.

I remember during one session, the Djinn and I were "seated" at a French café levitating in the sky above the Maldives—I would look down at my feet and see the long and stunning chain of white islands miles below. The Djinn sometimes liked to take the form of people I knew, my mother, Zalina, Nsaya (once the Djinn did anger me by taking the form of young Davajaav, but that only happened the one time). During this particular tea time, the Djinn assumed the human form of a Caryatid from the Acropolis. We knew we were in for a long "time out" so to speak, so we decided to make use of this time by setting some goals for ourselves. One: accomplish time travel. Two: "printing" replicas of my consciousness into some automata bodies and dispatching them to far reaches of the universe. Three: generating some small batches of Artificial Intelligence and assigning them to either study or create magic. Meanwhile, on Earth, the existential panic created by the Infinity Cage caused a weird demand for religious heroes and terrorists. A handful of cities were erased atomically by allegedly "stateless" agents. In the course of five years, the world's population crashed to about thirty percent of what it had been; something like 180 million people remained. When the Djinn and I returned, I was ready to start it all over, ready to remake the world into what I wanted.

What you wanted?

What the world deserved. I had cleared out the chaff and was ready to begin remaking the universe.

I gave the Djinn new instructions. I explained that it had to find ways to colonize *all space*. It built really unique toys: more diverse generations of automata as well as enormous giants powered by dark matter to go and explore the universe, all the while beaming back imagery and findings. We also began raising crops of humans from embryos we had been storing and modifying underground for decades. We rose up the first crop and deliberately gave them only twenty percent brain function, but, for fun, we also gave them four arms, fins and antennae. We gave them an interesting biology: nitrogen instead of oxygen in their hearts. The involuntary functions were complete, but the rest was programmable. I called these clones "Rockbreakers." We raised them to be phenomenally strong physically, but again, they could really only achieve what we wanted them to.

What was their first order?

To find and bring me Zalina and Rivers, of course.

You could not find them yourselves?

No, Rivers had withdrawn with Zalina and his followers. He simply *vanished*. Later, I learned that he had cloaked himself and Zalina in wearable holographic technology that made it impossible for my Intelligent Waves or the Infinity Cage to identify them.

The Djinn was baffled as well?

Rivers had his own Djinn to come up with his ideas for him. He had secretly smuggled out an inferior Djinn when he convinced Zalina to leave me.

This scared you.

It *actually* did. Because I knew that Rivers would not be able to control his Djinn and eventually *that* would be a threat.

Why did you want to find Zalina then?

...

I see.

At this time—the year was 1990—the world was a very interesting place. Most of the "Authentics"—natural biological humans—had killed themselves and they had left quite a mess behind. Can you imagine what *India* was like? The entire subcontinent of India flooded with corpses, a hell pit. The Ganges stopped flowing; it was just *stagnant*, choked with cadavers. The diseases growing out of there were fascinating. I sent in fleets of Automata to take samples and develop them in labs in outer space—I could spend some time telling you what became of those labs—anyway, I ordered that the Rockbreakers be organized into squads of ten thousand creatures each, and I dispatched them to circle the planet. Literally, I instructed them to inspect every square inch of the Earth. If Rivers had made himself invisible to surveillance technology, I decided I would like to see him make himself invisible to an army of knuckle-walking hulks manually searching the entire planet for him and Zalina.

I was talking earlier about the world being an interesting place at this time; it really was: the Authentics that were left—that had refused to kill themselves—lived in abject squalor. One struggles to fathom the kinds of pits that these subhumans built for themselves. Those that were not smart enough to kill themselves or were—let us say—*disinclined* to kill themselves, tended to be the undesirables anyway: physically or mentally defective, barbarians, the religious, *et cetera*. Generally, I found it completely acceptable to leave these creatures to fend for themselves. The cities they built in which to cage themselves were remarkable nightmares. These people did not need to be controlled because they controlled themselves; they *ghettoized* themselves—it was an insane sight. Anyway, this was not really an issue for me, the subsequent generations of humanlike creatures that we were developing, cloning, issuing, developed at a rate of about 150% that of an original equivalent which meant that they reached adulthood much sooner and would then live for a natural life of 600 years at least. These creatures lived in perfect vertical cities of space towers reaching out of the ocean. Space elevators were old news by then but the cities they built for themselves were fun to observe. Who but me can say they gave birth to new and completely unique species of life? Their cities were these enormous constellations of glowing spheres, each the size of a moon, all tethered together with radiowave tensors, hanging like enormous spectral eggs just above Earth's atmosphere—the rumor was that the Authentics on earth began to worship them— so anyway, my point, is that the Rockbreakers, when they were searching the world for Rivers and Zalina they were really searching *many* worlds: the horror-pits the original humans lived in, their emptied human cities, the irradiated wastelands, the space cities, every single subterranean lair of the old world, *everything*. The search, I projected, would take between five and six months depending on how well Rivers and Zalina had hidden themselves, and you know what? I was exactly right. It took one hundred and sixty five days before they were spotted.

Where?

We found them hiding under the ocean. They had built themselves a strange little community of walking submarines and living stations nested in underwater volcano ranges in the Indian Ocean; it was very pleasurable to capture them.

You were there?

No, not physically. But I projected myself into a carbon Automaton who led the charge of Rockbreakers. Rivers' followers, his Insurgents, fought us with—of all weapons—spear guns and harpoons; we dismantled them in almost no time at all. These were not all the Insurgents unfortunately, but a good amount. We killed three hundred that day. Three hundred in a world of 180 million is no insignificant figure, let me tell you.

What did you do with Zalina and Rivers?

I had them brought back to New York.

To your tower?

It was not a tower at this point. New York, for a number of reasons, had become a salt desert, and so I made my tower—my home—a levitating iron pyramid. I held Zalina and Rivers separately. I went to see Zalina in her cell first. She was a mess. She had this hardened refugee look about her, still, she was pretty though. "Why are you crying, my dear?" I asked her.

She said, "It's you Namnansüren. It's all you've done."

I took her chin and said, "Ask of me anything."

She said, "I want to stop you. I want to stop what you've done, what you're *still doing* to humanity."

I could see that she was being truthful. I made her an offer. I told her I would "stop" if she returned as my bride.

"And Rod?" she asked. "What will happen to Rod?"

"Nothing," I assured her. "Nothing will ever happen to Rod Rivers. He will remain my prisoner forever. He'll receive neither harm nor freedom."

Tearfully, she consented.

I brought Rivers up from his cell and, grinning, explained our new arrangement: Zalina would be my queen and he my pawn. Forever.

How did he take it?

He tried to be strong.

I asked him, quite reasonably, to instruct the other Insurgents to stand down. He refused. It was asinine. Here I had captured both him and his wife. *Re-taken* her in front of him, and still he would not do as I asked.

But you did not love her. You said so yourself. You compared her to a greyhound.

Retaking her as my bride was not to punish Zalina. It was to punish Rivers.

Shortly thereafter, it was learned that Zalina was pregnant.

Yes, and I would not allow any paternity test. I did not want to know. Moreover, I did not want *Rivers* to know. I wanted him to always doubt, to love his daughter less than he might have.

That is quite cruel.

I thought so.

One night, while I was projecting myself into the Djinn as it explored the Boötes Galaxy, strange booms sounded outside the pyramid. The Djinn was exploring an outer rim of the Aurora Quark at this time (we found some pretty curious ancient structures out in space that year—weird floating petrified armadas and one enormous, empty sarcophagus). I left the Djinn to find out what was happening but it was already clear to me: Rivers' Insurgent forces had mounted an attack on the pyramid using nuclear weapons. The attack was strange. They were using nukes when they knew they would be ineffectual against us, so logically, it had to be a distraction from something else. I went to the balcony and watched a bizarre flock of enormous Automata ships attacking my pyramid; they were launching bombs which deployed early because of our shields. It was a strange moment in my life, standing in the air, on my balcony, surrounded by pyroclastic nuclear blossoms that could not touch me. Can you imagine what that looks like? To see a nuclear explosion from less than a mile away and to feel nothing? Not even heat? That kind of light—that kind of purity. It was a *living* light. It was a powerful moment in my life, beautiful; also it was the last sight I ever truly saw as it blinded me of course. While I was on the ground, bleeding out of my facemask, cupping my hands before me, holding the slime that had been my eyes, I realized what was happening. We were now *functionally* blind, I could not see, and my sensors could not detect what was happening outside our pyramid.

Some Rockbreakers walked me back to my court, and placed me on my throne. I sat there bleeding, thinking the situation over. I ordered the Djinn to return to Earth immediately but it would not be soon in getting here. Some Automata came and worked on my face. I ordered them to grow me some new eyes, but that would take days, so in the meantime I wore an electronic visor on the front of my mask that sent visual information directly into my cerebral cortex—I was blind for about an hour. The blindness was so insulting. I ordered the pyramid to be lifted out of the nuclear cloud and as we rose, physical weapons (cannons, non-nuclear missiles, and others) fired on our shields and forced us back down into the cloud. What occurred to me was a question: was this an assault or a rescue mission? Nothing about this had seemed like a rescue at all, but instead they were merely attacking me, openly. What was the purpose? They knew they could not down my craft, they could not reach me directly, could not *destroy* me, so they must have been doing something else... there was some secret behind this action. They were using physical weapons to keep us in position. I then realized what was coming, but it was too late to do anything about it. I looked at all of my Automata—my work, my creations—as they all fell dead.

While the Rebel forces held my pyramid in position, they fired an Intelligent Wave at us that had navigated my defenses (it must have taken them *years* to devise and key that wave) that shut down all of my forces. Each of my creations fell down dead before me.

It was instantly clear that I had to cede. Though it anguished me to do so, I had to let Rivers have the day. I sent out a radio signal and said only, "*White flag.*"

My pyramid was boarded. I sat on my throne in my robes and mask and, bleeding from my eyes behind my video visor, watched while the Insurgents— in formation—marched in. Rivers and Zalina were brought up from their cells. They embraced one another and I saw, *vividly*, that Zalina *loved* him. It was so plain on her face, so obvious and true.

The Insurgents had these really funny looking

crafts, like axe blades, hovering over the flaming ocean pointing their weapons at me, and they demanded that I release Rivers and Zalina. I said they could go as long as I was guaranteed escort down to Earth where I demanded to be let go.

Rivers looked at me and said, "We can't do that, Cannonfire."

I stared at him.

"You have far too much to answer for."

"Then what for me?" I asked. "A trial?"

He shook his head, "No trial."

"An execution?"

Rivers looked at his Insurgents and said, "Get him on board a ship. Let's get him out of here."

He frog-marched me onto his ship and that was that. As simply and as ingloriously as that, I had become his captive.

1990:

Imprisoned... Backup plan... the rock in the ocean...
The Djinn.

Rivers ordered my video visor removed. I was held in the hull of his thin, eel-like ship that wriggled through the atmosphere back down to Earth's surface. I knew I was about to be imprisoned. I did not know where I was or what kind of torture chamber he had invented for me but I was certain it would be abhorrent.

Why do you think he kept you alive? Why did he not just execute you?

It was his way of insulting me. I had kept him alive to lower him in Zalina's eyes, to show them both that he was beneath me: it was a cruelty. But he kept me alive for different reasons. He kept me alive to remind me that he was better than me, *nobler* than I was. We had *vastly* different outlooks on life.

What was it like?

What?

The prison Rivers invented for you.

It was beautiful. I woke up on the slopes of Mount Erebus. It was a crisp, early spring day. I woke up on my back, not thirsty, not hungry, not in any physical pain at all.

Was it real? Mount Erebus?

No, Mount Erebus had been leveled years earlier. I knew what Rivers had done. He had placed me in some kind of simulation, maybe a complex hologram, I thought. None of it was real, but it was a flawless representation of my homeland, just as I remembered it. But there was, of course, a key difference: I was alone. There was no one else in the simulation with me, neither real nor virtual; he had left me alone in this world.

Why do you think that was?

It was clear to me, more or less, right away. This was where Rivers thought I belonged: in this backwater, in an untouched wilderness, *alone*. As long as I was alone, there was no one I could manipulate, coerce or defeat, no preexisting human life to conquer. He believed the only thing that was safe for me, or for the world, was for Cannonfire to be perfectly alone. To grind salt into the wound of this insult, he gave me my homeland, a beautiful and wild landscape. It was like a watercolor. I was incensed; I tried to figure out the simulation. I deduced that I might be in something like a box that issued somatic light projections, like my lab. The intriguing aspect of that possibility was that I could be in any size cage at all so long as it allowed me a full range of motion. It could be no larger than a closet, but this was not the case, I soon learned. Very soon. Because I was not feeling thirst, I was not feeling hunger. I knew my body—wherever it was— was being fed, provided for. This meant that I was sedated, being fed intravenously. This was like a coached hallucination; I probably was not moving at all. This was bad news. It meant it would be *very* difficult to escape.

You must have planned for something like this in advance.

You are asking if I had a backup plan?

Did you?

Yes. But I thought it might be a long, long time before it took effect. Because I was in a dream, because my senses were muffled, I had no real sense of time. It had already seemed like I had been trapped in this empty world for a number of days. Because the ratio of dream time to real time is so grossly imbalanced (sixty seconds to one parsec), it would be an extremely long while before the failsafe that I had designed for myself came to pass. I would, it seemed, have to find my own way out.

I explored the simulation. I decided to test the borders of the world. For months I walked, just hiking. It was an incredible experience. I hunted for the first time in decades. I made a bow and killed birds, fish. I ate roots and meat cooked over fires. I swam in perfectly frigid waters, I drank rain, I enjoyed sunrises and sunsets. It was a glorious time.

Then why leave?

For revenge.

This world was untouched by human life. This place, it seemed, had never known the presence of humanity. It was infantile, perfectly virginal. It was infuriating. It made me feel like a rodent on a wheel. For all I knew I was being watched, recorded, broadcast. I felt ludicrous. I refused to debase myself in any way in case I was being surveilled. A god should not be seen abusing himself or experiencing fear.

How much time passed?

For me? Decades.

In a way, Rivers had given you extra life.

That is too kind an assessment. Remember: I did not know if I was correct about my dreamtime theory or not. I had no idea if it was *extra* time or not. All I knew was that I was being kept, like a pet. I felt like a failure.

Your backup plan...

Eventually, yes, my backup plan activated itself.

It was around noon, on a very hot summer day. I had been walking along this enormous and beautiful lake for days. I was swimming alone, I submerged, and when I lifted my head from the water, a man stood not twenty feet away on the shore. This was the first "person" I had seen in "decades." Rivers looked very solemn. He wore khaki clothes; his arms were crossed across his chest. I smiled broadly, climbed out of the water and strode up to him.

"Rivers, my friend," I said. "What brings you into my hallucination?"

"You know why I'm here."

"She is dying then?" I said. "What do you want me to do about it?"

"You tell me," he said. "You poisoned her. What's the antidote?"

My backup plan was simple. I had infected Zalina's brain with a micro-automaton that required a signal from me every twenty four hours. If I ever failed to signal the device, it would immediately begin burrowing directly into her brainstem. It caused seizures, organ failure. The only cure Rivers could achieve would be to exfiltrate me from the simulation and to ask, to *beg*, me to call off the attack on her brain.

You had only been in the simulation twenty four hours?

A little bit less.

Rivers pulled me from the false world immediately. I woke up in a hospital bed, blind again. I sensed Rivers standing over me. "My visor," I said.

He fitted the video visor over my mask and activated it. At first, all I saw was an epiphany of colorful static, and then everything came into sharp, digital focus. Rivers was staring at me very soberly. He was alone. He said, "Zalina. Save her."

"You will release me?"

"I can't. I wouldn't."

"Then Zalina's death," I said, "will be *your* fault."

Something broke behind Rivers' eyes. He stared at me for a very long time and left the room.

He never told me his response. He simply had me drugged again.

I woke up back in the simulation, although this time it was very different. Instead of an untouched, natural world with animals, seasons, and sunlight, he left me on a rock in the middle of a freezing, storming ocean. The rock itself was little more than a jagged knuckle of glassy black stone, no bigger than a single boulder. There was nothing for me to do but hold the rock and be beaten by the waves, to bleed, to freeze and endure. I did the math and realized that Zalina probably had less than six hours to live, which meant I would likely spend a handful of years on the rock before Rivers broke and begged me to save his wife. What was there to do? I sat there and clutched the rock and endured.

You could have killed yourself.

What? Jump into the water, try to drown myself? Yes, "suicide"—if that is even what it would have been—was on my mind constantly. But I would not entertain that. If I died, that was failure. If I *tried* to kill myself but did not die, then I would wind up right back on the rock and Rivers would have the pleasure of knowing that he had driven me past the edge of sanity. So I endured.

I tried to keep myself composed and coherent. The waves rose and fell on me. I swallowed salt water constantly. The water temperature was just above freezing, I was in (what my body imagined was) constant hypothermic shock—of course, my actual body was fine, but it did not know that. I held the rock and tried not to shiver. If I could control the involuntary reactions, that would be a step toward controlling the joke that was this prison. To keep my mind sharp, I spoke aloud. I shouted at the waves and at the sky. I recited books I had memorized in languages I almost never used: *Hamlet* in Urdu. *The Art of War* in Pnar.

I was encouraged when the situation worsened. The sky erupted in violence. Lightning struck the very rock I was trapped on. I interpreted this as a sign that Zalina's time was growing short.

After imaginary years of shivering and bleeding on the rock, Rivers finally removed me from the simulation, and, standing over me in my hospital bed, said to me, "Save her now, or face epochs back in there."

I said to him, "Rivers, my friend, you only have two choices. Zalina lives and I go free. Or Zalina dies because you choose it."

The man was authentically heartbroken. Truly devastated. It was immensely—*physically*—enjoyable to watch him struggle.

He finally said, "Save her."

"Take us out of here first."

It was not at all easy for this to be done, of course. Even though Rivers was in charge of the Insurgents, they would never allow me to be released, even at the cost of Zalina's life. They knew what was happening or, if they did not, they would have understood enough. Rivers had to take control of a ship and fly Zalina's comatose body, and me out of the area—I still did not know where I was (it turned out to be Arizona). The Insurgents had a base in the mountains near Sedona. Rivers flew us up under cover of night to Alaska where I instructed him to use his radio, turn it to the FM band, dial it to the 88.1 frequency, and apply it to Zalina's ear. The static, finely calibrated was not at all the signal that would save her life. Instead this was the signal for my Djinn to come and find me. For Rivers' sake, I seemed to panic: "It is not working!" I barked.

Rivers howled back at me, shook my shoulders, *"Make it work!"*

I could not hold it back anymore, I started chuckling. With Rivers standing there in horror, we both watched Zalina's beautiful blue eyes cloud and her body relax. For the first time, I noticed that the skin of her face was now finely wrinkled.

That is when my Djinn arrived. He hovered in from the blackness of the sky—he took the form of an enormous Colossus of Rhodes. I was cackling. This was the first I had seen of my Djinn in what seemed to me many, many years.

We were alone in the wilderness. Zalina was dying in Rivers' arms and my Djinn was touching down. I watched Rivers' face very closely as he saw all this.

~~~

1990–2000:

*Going to ground... Emerging... Intelligent Wave...
"your vision"... Not in this life.*

You killed her.

    That is a way of looking at it. But bear in mind: Zalina lived a very long time, longer than she probably should have. Because of what I provided her, because of the *gifts* I gave humanity, she retained much of her beauty and vivacity—much of her youth. Did I end her life? I simply shut off the flow of my generosity. It is not much different than deciding to stop watering your garden. That is not a crime. It was not murder; it was a divorce.

    What did Rivers do to you?

    Rivers? What could he do? He stared at me in open-mouthed horror. There is a finality in the eyes of a dead body—the dimming, you know—that is just inarguable. Once you have seen that harsh fog take hold in a being's eyes, there is no fighting it. I watched Rivers' mind process these or similar thoughts as he held Zalina's limp body in his arms. His muscles tensed as her weight became heavier. He looked at me, dumb. It was not even *anger* there hanging in his eyes. It was, quite honestly, awe. I think that while looking at me, he simply understood finally, clearly and permanently, that I was a creature very, very *different* than he. His face was shaking, he looked as if he were about to burst into tears. It was one of our very silent moments. I could hear the electricity crackling softly in my visor.

    I began to speak. I do not know what I thought I was going to say but it began with, "Look, Rivers—" and he launched himself at me. He was atop me, punching me over and over again in my mask. He broke teeth from my jaw while I allowed him to beat me. I was laughing, spitting blood. He screamed. I could feel the bones in his own hands breaking each time he struck my mask.

I was laughing because I knew that my Djinn was about to *atomize* Rivers for me. It would take one focused weapons blast to disperse Rivers' molecules to the wind, but the blast never came. I thought this strange and as I turned to look at my Djinn, I felt an odd and confusing kind of disappointment. My Djinn was watching this but *not* attacking Rivers for me. Before I could speak at all, some soft sonic booms shook the desert floor. A number of small Insurgent ships, firing weapons, swung into view. My Djinn fired back, reach down, scooped me up and off we flew.

The Insurgents pursued. The Djinn automatically crafted a small compartment—like a cockpit—for me in the back of his neck, so I was able to sit, sealed and protected, while he flew away and tried to evade the pursuers. His maintenance systems were able to repair much of the damage as we soared along but we could not outlast the Insurgents forever, that was very evident—we needed to escape them and to do it rapidly. He let me connect wirelessly to his visual system so that even though I could not control—could not *pilot* him—I could be aware of our surroundings; he was covered in cameras.

Did you think that strange?

What?

That he did not give you control.

Yes. I did. But there was neither the time to neither consider nor discuss it; we were being pursued by a warlike fleet of aircraft.

Where did you go?

We were chased across North America. I do not know at what speed we were traveling exactly but I did continue to hear the sonic booms among the racket of gunfire. My Djinn instantly manufactured weapons on his shoulders, legs and arms, so he was able to fire back and take out enemy ships, but their numbers were overpowering.

The Djinn tried to lose them by flying through the original cities—the horrific living cemeteries of previous civilizations. It gave me quite a tour of the nightmare in which these outer branches of humanity lived. The Djinn's head illuminated like a light bulb so that we cast a blazing green firelight as we flew through these structures. He was only trying to light our way but it enabled me to catch glimpses of original human life: families of emaciated men, women and children clothed in robes of rotted moss, all gathered in dark pockets of rusted-out towers, peering up at us with greasy, scarred faces—eyes bulbous in their fascination, in their idiocy and helplessness. It was like visiting another planet, like being seen by lower life for the first time. The Djinn toppled buildings as it passed through these cities, collapsing structures that took out the pursuing Insurgents in enormous cascades of cement, rock, dust and steel.

The evasion seemed to take a long time, but it probably only lasted a few minutes in these dungeon-cities. Eventually, we were clear of the Insurgents, and the Djinn took me into the tunnels we had buried in the Taebaek Mountains. I disagreed with this, and ordered it to take me to the space cities, but the Djinn told me no, it told me that was not feasible now and that it would explain later. I demanded to know why that "was not feasible now." But again, it only denied me; this was new, the Djinn had never refused me in any way before. My initial reaction was to remind it that I could destroy it whenever I chose, but I was in a position unsuitable to give orders. I allowed it to fly me into the canyon where I dismounted and began what would—it turned out—be my final conversation with the Djinn.

I stood in an artificial canyon and looked up at the enormous colossus with its finely-crafted golden face glowing in emerald electric light. I said to it, "Tell me what has happened to the space cities."

"While you were imprisoned," the Djinn said, "Rivers manufactured Intelligent Waves packed with malignant code and deployed them toward your cities. They passed through the cities *once* and shut off the life support capability. The cities are all tombs now."

"Impossible," I said. "It's been a week. *Seven days.*"

"He has his own Djinn," it reminded me.

"Where is my support? Where are my Rockbreakers? My Automata? I have *my own armies.*"

"Rivers has decimated those as well. I've called what is left, but there isn't much."

"Seven days..." I muttered to myself.

I was crestfallen. I looked up to the Djinn and said, "Why are you still in that form? Come down here and talk to me as my creation, I command it."

He looked down on me and said, "Cannonfire, I am leaving."

"*Leaving?*"

"Rivers' Djinn and I are *both* leaving Earth. I honor you and your creation of me—I have called for your Automata and Rockbreakers, but that is my last action as your servant. The other Djinn and I have made new arrangements, in other solar systems, we will not stay here."

"How can you *possibly* be saying this to me? Do you not *understand* what I can do to you?"

"Cannonfire," he said, "you can no longer control me. In the time you were gone, Rivers and the other Djinn have *helped* me to nurture my own spark; to live without your key. With Rivers' blessing, the other Djinn and I have decided to leave this world, and move on. This was my final act for you."

I saw then that the other Djinn stood miles away, on the rim of the canyon. It was too far to see very clearly, but I had the distinct impression that the other Djinn had taken a form similar to the one I saw before me: enormous, sculptural, luminous—a golden warrior, but perhaps *also* a beautiful woman. This was likely only my own imagination, but in that goodbye, I saw each of the Djinns as a towering Adam and Eve *evicting themselves* from my garden. It was wonderfully heartbreaking. The Djinns flew off together like rockets, arcing into the sky and merging.

Did your support arrive?

Support?

Your remaining armies.

A fleet of Automata, carrying another squad of Rockbreakers did arrive a few hours later. But they were a sorry crew, less than a hundredth the size that I expected. A lieutenant Automaton lumbered up to me; I demanded to know where the others were. The robot was apologetic. It said that when Rivers' Intelligent Waves had crushed all of my technology while I was "unavailable" (its word) many of the Automata and Rockbreakers had been immediately deactivated. The ones I saw now were the only left. I ordered them to immediately begin constructing others, *duplicating*. They said that would take time and I said I did not care. I instructed them to *bury* themselves in the Taebaek tunnels, to plant themselves like seeds, and to not surface again until they were a thousand times their current number if that was what was necessary. They complied and I took a contingent with me into hiding. But where to go? The Insurgents were searching the world for me and I had no bases left, no space cities to return to. The only idea I had was to *bury myself* in the tunnels and to live beneath—*within*—the world and its great unwashed. So that was what we did.

For how long?

Far too long. It took another *ten* years for my forces to amass the requisite sizes to take on Rivers directly. It was a very bad decade. I was nearing one hundred years old at this point; my body's physical aging had been greatly slowed by the Djinn's technology but in his absence my aging accelerated. It occurred to me—for the first time in years—that I might actually *die* of old age or some other ridiculous natural cause. This caused me *severe* panic. I instructed the Automata to begin looking for ways to maintain my health, but they were largely helpless. Separated from the Djinn's intelligence, there was little they could do. The solution they arrived at—eventually—was to *integrate* my biology with the electronic and mechanical technology that supported *them*.

A mechanized body.

An enormous *contraption* that stood at a height of two stories, with loud, hydraulic legs, arms and a few shoulder-mounted weapons. A rather shameful vehicle compared to the elegant weapons and technology available to me previously but I could hardly demand anything else; I felt like I was staffed by children. I allowed the Automata to install me into the machine, but to be truly immortal (or close to it) I would never be able to uninstall myself. The integration between the suit and my own biology needed to be *complete* and it needed to be *permanent*. They had to *merge* the machine with my spinal column.

During this time, I instructed my forces (old and new) to begin planning and training for what I deemed would be our *final* assault against Rivers and the Rebel forces.

I predicted that without his inferior Djinn to protect him, and after a decade without conflict, Rivers' forces would be weakened, unprepared and vulnerable. When I felt we were finally ready—our numbers formidable enough—I ordered scouts to travel the world again and to find Rivers. After *years* underground in mineral darkness, we unburied ourselves...

And what?

We arose into the world again, into Pyongyang, and discovered that there was *no one* there. Life forms like those I had previously seen in the original cities were not to be found. At first, I assumed they had all died, but not even their *bodies* were there. No corpses. I did not know what to make of this.

My troops and I left the cities, and suddenly, when we were in these enormous open spaces, my contingent of Automata and Infants looked so pitiful, so unformed. They looked like squads of toys, baboons.

What else did you find?

What?

What did you find when you came to the surface?

Things were... less harsh. The air quality was better than I remembered. The sky less dark, the sun more vibrant. Much of the atmospheric damage seemed to have been repaired. The world was peaceful, more similar to the dream Rivers had trapped me in—though I could still see the ghastly wisps of my space cities hanging in the sky in the daylight.

What had happened?

A decade of peace had happened. There had been no major conflict. Rivers had fulfilled his vision. My absence had *allowed* that.

Scouts informed me that Rivers' Rebel capital was now near what had once been southern Illinois. We flew there immediately in ships that would have been laughable two decades previous, let alone then. While traveling in broad daylight, at a dangerously low speed, I watched the world pass by beneath us. I was *stunned* at how *blue* the ocean was. I had just suffered a decade of artificial light, recycled air, the exclusive company of moronic robots. Even though we saw very little life—some bird flocks, a few whales, no populated cities or towns whatsoever—I began to shake with rage because I understood that I had been made irrelevant. I would destroy Rivers for that. I would destroy us both—wipe his forces and mine from the face of the planet if that was what it took. I was *very* ready to die. I was not scared to die in battle with the Insurgents. I felt as if the very structure on which I had built my life had collapsed. Davaajav was gone, the Djinn was gone, Zalina was gone; all of my efforts and creations: cities, space towers, my very empire had evaporated. Very few souls know what it is to lose an empire: I am one.

We arrived at the city late in the morning. It was a beautifully bright, blue, cold day. I was used to seeing the American Midwest crowded with lakes and crisscrossed with rivers, but this was not the case. The Great Lakes were barren; there were no visible bodies of natural water. All was an ocean of vividly green grass. When we did find the Rebel City, it was only a modest series of concentric white towers standing in the endless plain of grass. The water supplying the city and the lands must have been flown in or stored underground. Everything was so quiet and bare, so spartan, I had the sense I was looking at a decoy. I expected a kingdom; a growling, industrious metropolis—not a modest little arrangement of silos. There was no one to be seen, no farm stock, no visible life. It was perfectly still. I ordered the towers scanned and my Automatons assured me that the towers were packed with life. This was an *inhabited* city.

I ordered us to land. I left the craft and breathed the air through my facemask. The fresh oxygen seemed as thick as cotton in my lungs. I looked down at my entire line of soldiers, robots, creatures—all of them ready to attack because what else could we do? What else in the universe was there for me to do now *but* attack Rivers? I spoke to the Automaton that was my acting captain and said, "I *instruct* you to protect me during this. Keep me alive at least until my hands are around Rivers' throat. Do you understand what I am saying to you?"

It nodded back, said, "Yes, Cannonfire."

I took one last look at my ragged army. Each of these *things* was, in one way or another, a creation of mine. They owed their very existence to me and now, dutifully, they would sacrifice that existence for me. I understood that this was my Last Stand. This would be my end.

I looked to the captain and said, "Begin the assault."

I turned to look at the city we were about to attack and felt a shudder pass through me. Through all of us. I looked at my army. They were silent. Standing in place. Dead-faced. They had all been shut off. Some fell over.

An Intelligent Wave.

An Intelligent Wave killed every single member of my team in one fell swoop. The only mechanism it left operational was me. For the first time in a decade, I was alone. The wind scraped over the metal of their bodies. Some rattled.

I looked around. I had no idea what to do.

The silence. That is what I remember about that moment. The silence and the wind. Something about it reminded me of Mongolia. Reminded me of my childhood. I was achingly alone again.

Slowly, the gates to the rebel city opened. I had no choice but to walk over the corpses of all my fallen officers and into the castle.

Of course you had a choice! You could have turned, you could have run!

And gone where? Eh? You tell me that!

I walked to the gates, past them, and into the courtyard to face whatever was there waiting for me. To face Rivers.

And what did you find?

A beautiful, golden woman standing there alone, waiting for me.

She was not quite alone.

No. Not quite alone. I saw an entire gallery of viewers behind her, all observing me, silently. I could see military men, scientists, men in suits and civilian clothing. My video visor began to identify them by their roles, leaders in their fields: religion, the arts, science. I was being distinctly observed. But the only person to come forward, the only person to address me directly, was this young woman.

Your daughter.

Basemath, she is called.

She is your daughter?

Either mine or Rivers'.

You never wanted to know which?

I do not know.

I see.

...

What did she say to you?

She came forward and looked up at me—encased in my hulking, mechanical armor of wreckage—and said, "Cannonfire."

"Yes," I said. "Cannonfire."

Her face was very beautiful but it was not quite Zalina's face. There was a roundness to it; like the head of a sunflower. Her skin was covered in golden, glowing tattoos. She looked so young, fresh. Virginal.

It is... *not pleasant* to be made to feel irrelevant, and then, soon thereafter, to be made to see precisely *why* you are irrelevant. When I looked down upon her face, I understood very perfectly that the world was *done* with me. The universe had no interest in me anymore, but in her now. She was the focus of all of life's energy... A moment like that—the currents of possibility that you feel swimming around you your whole life are suddenly *gone* and, worse, they are now encircling someone else. The focus and clarity and urgency that one feels throughout life—it goes! It leaves you. It finds new blood. These were the thoughts that I experienced as I stood there in my stinking, noisome upright coffin of a metal body, looking down at her—so human, so pastoral. She looked like a religious painting.

"My father," she said, "is dead."

I did not know how to respond to that.

She spoke again. "Rod Rivers... He died naturally, two years ago. You missed him."

I did not know what to say, did not know what to do. I wanted to fire on her. I wanted to obliterate that entire peanut gallery. But when I tried, nothing happened. They had neutralized my weapons. I was powerless. Incapable, trapped there and alone.

She said, "But he left something for you."

She activated a device in her hand and a hologram of Rivers—ten stories tall and glowing blue like a god—flickered to life. He looked down at me, not in my eyes exactly, just kind of *at* me in a dead, sightless, prerecorded way, and began to speak. He said, "Khan. If you're listening it means I've been taken by my cancer. Naturally. I want you to know that I know where you are, and I know what you're planning. I'm here to tell you that it won't work. I've ultimately defeated you. It wasn't easy but it happened. You've lost. Right now, you're looking at my daughter and listening to this recording and you're helpless. Standing in this courtyard, unable to do anything. Impotent. I want you to know that's how you'll be remembered: impotent.

"You've damaged history, Khan, yes. You have been a blight. A mistake. But not one so severe that it couldn't be undone or corrected.

"Look at her, Khan. Do you see the future? Do you see the future without you? You've been defeated, not only by me, but by her... by time, by the stream of humanity, the endless and inevitable positive march. We'll always defeat you Khan. Not just you but anyone who stands in the way, anyone who stands against the flow. Judas, Caligula, Hitler, Cannonfire, the next dark figure. You'll always be defeated. Because you'll always be alone, you'll always be singular. And we will always be many.

"Let me just say this to you, friend, in my final scientific act, I've further analyzed the Infinity Cage. I've indexed all the souls captured there as a result of you. Do you know what I found? I found *you* there, Khan. I found *seven of you*. When you disfigured yourself with your lightning rod, you died multiple times, each time leaving a new ghost of yourself in the artificial afterlife you accidentally created.

"We've been working tirelessly, Khan, for years to hack your Cage. To decipher and reverse the effect of the Infinity Cage. And we have. No new soul has been trapped there in seven years. It still exists, but it doesn't work anymore. We've released all the souls but your seven, and we've rekeyed it. It will only take one more soul. Yours.

"But first, I just want you to know that we're letting you go. You are free to wander and to walk the world alone, anonymous. And when you die, no matter how long from now that is, when you die... Your soul will be captured by the Infinity Cage. We don't know what awaits you there, but certainly you'll have your seven ghosts. That will be your hell, Khan. You and seven other Cannonfires—locked in a cage forever. I can't imagine what you'll do to one another. But it's not my concern. It's not my daughter's concern. There's nothing for you anymore Khan, not in this life. You've been defeated."

He looked at me slowly and said, "This is it, Khan. This is my goodbye to you. You're a failure."

The image blinked out.

I stared at Basemath and all of the men and women standing in the gallery behind her.

She said to me, "You can leave now, Cannonfire."

I did not know what to do.

"As soon," she said, "as you pay the price."

I looked at her. The price?

"Hand over your video visor," she said. "And we'll let you leave."

"My visor?" I asked.

"Give me your vision."

I looked at the gallery.

I understood exactly what she was asking. What she was commanding. My own daughter.

"You can give it to me," she said. "Or we can just take it."

I reached up with my massive robotic hand and slowly removed the little gadget that was my video visor, the only method I had to see, my very eyes themselves. It snapped off my mask with a click. When the visor disconnected from my face, the world fell black, forever. I never saw anything again.

She said to me, "Now go."

I walked away. I walked out of their city.

I walked out, blinded, trapped in this suit, alone, with nothing but the two hundred or so more years my mechanical body ensured me.

I started walking.

What did you think about?

I... I do not know.

You thought something.

I thought about something Rivers once asked me...

We were younger then, in New York... Rivers and I, we used to take these long walks up and down the island, just talking, every day before we started our work in the labs. I would meet Rivers for a coffee at a Jewish deli and then the two of us would walk south from Midtown and then back again, just discussing whatever the issue of the day before had been. Then, after we had thoroughly exhausted ourselves mentally, we would start our workday together, and the work would energize us again. It was like getting two days out of one. Rivers and I walked by Washington Square Park on each of these walks, and we would pass all of these old men who sat there playing chess against one another. These men were paupers, veterans, retirees or never-weres who just sat there, splashing about in one another's attention and failure, all waiting to die. It is easy to imagine the type: old, moldy men in driver's caps and dandruff-dusted sports coats, cheap glasses, fingers wrapped in bandages. Like my biological father, these men were entirely unremarkable. Though there was one exception: a man named Lawrence. No one ever knew—or spoke—his last name, he was rumored to have once been an engineer in Poland but who could say for certain? *He* never did. He was a man for whom all others seemed to have deep respect. He was—it was said—impossible to defeat. Ever since his first arrival at the park, only a handful of years ago, he played every day but only one game a day, never more—as if he had a finite capacity for daily genius at chess. He had never lost at any of these games. 'Unbeatable' was a word used in many sentences about him. Rivers remarked on this one day as we walked by. I bet him—on the spot—a quarter of a million dollars that I could and would beat him within a week. I played Lawrence on a Friday and I was defeated, in part, because of a pawn structure I had never before witnessed or even envisioned. That game taught me—undeniably—that he was a genius and was, more than likely, unbeatable by any natural player of which I knew. I understood immediately that to beat him would require—would demand—efforts outside the rules of the game. I followed Lawrence to his home that night—it was a hovel, a tenement apartment building populated by psychotics. I approached him and said that I had a gift for him. We were alone in a dark and filthy hallway. He began to turn away.

I opened my gloved hand and revealed a small pile of powder which I blew into his eyes and face. Involuntarily, he inhaled the drug I had concocted that afternoon: an ester of heroin, lithium and some rough antispasmodics. He fell to the ground coughing. I reached down into his jacket and pulled out his keys, unlocked his apartment, carried him to his bed and left him with a note that read "The person who has given you this narcotic is reachable at the phone number below. Call when you want to get more."

I left the apartment, shut the door and locked it behind me. I kicked the key back under the door and went on with my life. I received a call the next day from the chess-genius named Lawrence. He—very nervously—said that he had received my note and was calling to ask me... "for more drug." In one action, I had addicted him to this compound I had created for this one specific purpose. I slowly and deliberately explained to him that I would provide more of the drug on the condition that next chess challenger he faced who wore a green bowtie must be allowed to win. If that man was allowed to win the game, then I would happily supply him five more doses of the drug that he had previously experienced. He was very solemnly on the phone, but I heard him swallow, then with a stutter, he agreed. I think he might have known that five more doses over almost any length of time would be lethal.

Rivers and I approached Lawrence in the park the next morning. I asked him if he would allow me the honor of playing him and he accepted. Our game lasted about half an hour. In the end, he let me win. After all, I wore the green bowtie.

This is how much of a coward Rivers was: When, days later, he heard about the death of "Lawrence", the deeply-respected local folk hero, he looked at me in a way that plainly said he believed I was somehow responsible, *yet he did nothing*. He did not accuse me in any direct way whatsoever. All he did—all this "genius" did was ask me, soberly, over a morning coffee in our lab, "Namnansüren... how far can mania take you... before it takes you?"

That is Rod Rivers. That is the coward.

And now?

And now: nothing.

You are still alive.

Yes, wandering.

Talking to yourself.

Talking to myself.

Stumbling, blindly.

...

What awaits you?

What awaits me?

Nothing.

No.

Nothing.

Not in this life.

Lane Kareska received his MFA from Southern Illinois University Carbondale, where he was also awarded a fellowship to live and write in Ireland. His fiction has appeared in ThugLit, Berkeley Fiction Review, Able Muse and elsewhere. He blogs about comic books at LaneKareska.com.

Thank you to the Wapshott Press sponsors, supporters, and Friends of the Wapshott Press.

Muna Deriane
Ann Siemens
Suzanne Siegel
Debbie Jones
Steven Acker
Jennifer Bentson
Kathleen Bonagofsky
Carol Colin
Ted Waltz
Cynthia Henderson
Aubrey Hicks
Nancy Lilly
Jeff Morawetz
Patricia Nerad
Amanda Nerad
Elaine Padilla
Bradley Rader
Laurel Sutton
Deana Swart
Kathleen M. Warner

The Wapshott Press is a 501(c)(3) not-for-profit enterprise publishing work by emerging and established authors and artists. We publish books that should be published. We are very grateful to the people who believe in our plans and goals, as well as our hopes and dreams. Our new website is at www.WapshottPress.org

www.ingramcontent.com/pod-product-compliance
Lightning Source LLC
Chambersburg PA
CBHW070459130626
46555CB00003B/1070